FOR LOVE OF THE EARL

JESSIE CLEVER

SOMEDAY LADY PUBLISHING, LLC.

For Mr. Cusimano
You told me I could. So I did.

CHAPTER 1

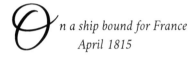*n a ship bound for France*
April 1815

SARAH SHOVED her elbow into him, pushing him farther against the wall. So Alec shoved back, sending his wife off the bunk and onto the grimy, disgusting floor of their prison on the ship bound for France. Alec closed his eyes and prayed to every god he knew for patience. His wife was going to come up fighting, and he would not be tempted to fight back. He was a gentleman, an earl, and earls did not box with their wives.

When he opened his eyes and looked at his wife, he felt his patience start a war with his temper.

Sarah looked furious. Her nostrils flared, and her hands fisted, ready to strike. Her lovely golden hair was clumped with seaweed and other unknown sea things, and her once pretty pink dress was covered in saltwater stains. The high lace collar was torn and hung limply down her heaving chest. Alec resolutely moved his gaze away from that heaving chest and up to her face, but then he found his gaze focused on her mouth with its delicious slight overbite.

He had tasted that mouth. But it had been in a fit of near rage and frustration and had been far too brief. He had tasted other parts of his wife as well, but again, it was a stolen taste that he now regretted. He would have apologized for it, but he suspected his wife would hit him. And he really didn't feel like having a broken nose.

"This is all your fault, you know," Sarah said, her teeth barely opening long enough to get the words out. Her nostrils flared with greater force.

Alec took a deep breath and sat up, swinging his legs to the side of the bunk. He ran his fingers over his face and through his hair, dislodging his own piece of seaweed. He looked at it before tossing it aside. He watched his feet slide around on the gunk on the floor as the ship rocked its way toward the Continent. The weak light from the lone lantern swinging from the rafters sent shadows dancing around the berth.

What was he going to say to his wife?

It seemed whenever he opened his mouth, she ripped out his tongue only to ram it back down his throat until he choked. So he looked up at her now, her beautiful face so full of hate, loathing really. Loathing him. And he looked at the floor again.

He did not know what to do. After four years, he still did not know how to make his wife believe that she was worth it. Worth everything. Worthy of being the wife of the Earl of Stryden. He just didn't know what to say or how to say it to her.

Alec Black, the Earl of Stryden, the son of the Duke of Lofton, and brilliant spy for the War Office, could not talk to his wife.

"I know," he finally whispered.

"If you hadn't taken off, your family would have been able to protect you. But you packed your things and left!" Sarah yelled now.

Alec raised a finger. "I did not pack. There wasn't time," he said and watched the loathing flare in her eyes.

He brought his finger down.

"Do you really wish to argue over semantics right now, my lord?"

Her tone had gone flat and smooth, the loathing searing into a blade of hate that pierced him just above his heart. Alec stopped pushing the gunk into piles on the floor with his boots. One of the piles looked suspiciously like the prime minister, which normally would have made Alec laugh, but laughing wasn't on his list of things to do just then.

"I know," he whispered again, this time not raising his head or a finger.

"Now you can't even look at me?" Sarah fumed.

Alec felt the need to swallow as four years of frustration boiled inside him. Looking at his shoes was not correct. Looking at her was not correct. Looking at her with love in his eyes was definitely not correct. So he raised his head with nothing but coldness in his eyes and looked at his wife.

But he didn't speak.

He really didn't feel like speaking again.

He might say something stupid like, I love you, I've always loved you, why can't we act like a real married couple and not like a the-War-Office-made-us-get-married couple, and why can't we make love all day long and only pause long enough sometime in the dark to eat little cucumber sandwiches with the crusts taken off in bed only to stop halfway through our snack to make love again until dawn when we finally collapse with words of love trailing off our exhausted lips?

Yes, he really shouldn't say that. His wife would castrate him with her bare hands. He crossed his legs.

"You really don't have anything to say?" Sarah asked, her voice suddenly, painfully quiet.

Alec shook his head negatively. He was not going to be tricked into saying what he was thinking. He had been thinking the same thing for four years, and it never changed no matter how he voiced his thoughts. How many times had he told Sarah that she was beautiful? That she was smart and witty and kind? And how many times had it not mattered?

Sarah threw her hands up in the air, and a guttural scream of rage tore from her throat. Alec looked back down at his shoes. He watched the shadows' dance be interrupted as Sarah paced the length of their prison. Five long shuffles of her feet up and five and half long shuffles back down to the door. The ship rolled unexpectedly, and Sarah's feet slid out from underneath her. Alec looked up too late to see her fall. Her head cracked against the wall of the small berth with a sickening thud. Alec tried to stand and ended up half scrambling across the slippery floor. He fell on his knees beside her, gently picking her up as his heart battered around in his chest.

"Sarah?"

He brushed her filthy hair out of her dirt-smudged face. Her eyes were closed, but her lips parted and soft words tumbled forth.

"Alec, don't leave me."

* * *

SEVERAL HOURS earlier on the English Channel

"YOU JUST HAD TO LEAVE, didn't you?" Sarah screamed over

the sound of the water coming over the side of the dinghy. She didn't catch the look on her husband's face. She was too busy not being swept into the Channel. The dinghy lurched suddenly, going deeper than it had before. Someone grabbed the back of her dress. She saw the surface of the water rise up precariously close to her face.

And she knew she didn't want to die.

She wanted to live a very long life. Preferably with her husband. She wanted babies, sons that had Alec's eyes, daughters who had his smile. She wanted to fight with her husband just to have the pleasure of making up with him. She just wanted life with him.

But he was going to leave. He had left. And right after very nearly, almost making love to her. It was cruel enough to just leave. He didn't have to leave during.

And all because she was a bastard, undeserving of a husband like the Earl of Stryden.

So that was why she seriously doubted she would be making babies with the man she loved so much it hurt. Earls did not make babies with orphans. Especially an orphan who had roots in a brothel.

The dinghy pitched again, and the hand holding the back of her dress tightened, dragging her backwards. She landed against her husband's chest. The wind rushed out of her as his other arm came around her, anchoring her to him. His lips were suddenly against her ear, and he spoke, but she wasn't sure if she was meant to hear it.

"I'm not losing you to the damn Channel."

Despite everything, she shivered. Shivered from his nearness, shivered from his words. Just shivered because it was him. And they were there. Surrounded by French sailors on their way to a ship that was going to take them to France, to the Comte de Montmartre, where they would be prisoners until someone came to rescue them. Although, if the comte's plan succeeded as the French wanted, then the comte would only be adding prisoners to his dungeon, not releasing any.

But right now her husband's arms were around her, and he didn't have to know how much she enjoyed that, wanted that. She could hide her response. After all, the Channel was attacking them. She doubted he would be paying much attention to how she reacted to his nearness. So for now, even though she was on a dinghy that could very well be swamped and she could very well be dragged to the bottom of the Channel, she was going to enjoy sitting in her husband's embrace, because it was very unlikely that she would ever be able to enjoy it again.

The dark blob on the horizon that was probably the ship they were being taken to didn't seem to grow. Sarah wondered if the sailors who were rowing were actually moving the boat. She leaned her head back, trying to get her lips against Alec's ear. Her mouth skimmed the rough stubble of beard along his jaw, and her toes clenched in her sodden slippers. Finally, her lips settled on his ear, and she could admit that they lingered longer than necessary before forming words.

"What are we going to do, now?" she asked.

She turned her head back around and tilted it, bringing her ear closer to his mouth. His lips were suddenly soft against her skin. She wondered if he might slip out his tongue to take a taste and almost shook her head to dislodge the thought, which would have sent her head into her husband's chin, and she doubted he would like that.

"We hope that Thatcher gets to Father in time."

Sarah turned her head around in the general direction of the shore as if she could see Thatcher there, riding off into the heart of England in search of another spy who could save them. But instead of the English coastline, she met the awful sneer of one of the French sailors. She raised her eyebrow at him, and the sailor started to rise. She swung her head around and burrowed deeper into Alec. His arm tightened immediately, which had her toes clenching again. She tilted her head back, this time resolutely ignoring the feeling that spiraled through her when her lips slipped over his skin.

"And what if he doesn't?"

They switched positions.

"We pray for a miracle."

Sarah swallowed. "How is he going to get to London that quickly?" she asked. "It took us days to get to Dover."

The wind blew Sarah's hair over her ear. She reached up to swipe it away and instead connected with Alec's hand, moving to do the same thing. Her eyes found his and locked. She thought maybe she should look away or at least blink, but she just stared at his green, green eyes. Blink, damn it. And finally she did. When she opened her eyes, Alec was frowning, and her stomach flipped in sudden dismay. She tilted her head obediently and waited for his answer.

"I think Father may be in Dover already after what Nathan and I learned when we found Samuel."

Sarah had nearly forgotten about that. It was true that she had tried to purposely block out some of the events that resulted from Samuel, the son of the infallible housekeeper Miss Eleanora Quinton, being kidnapped. But it had been days ago, probably weeks by now. It was getting hard to keep track of time, so she couldn't be sure. Samuel had been kidnapped right after Alec's brother, Nathan Black, had accidentally shot the brother of the man who was a spy for the French. Instead of shooting the spy, Lord Archer, Nathan had in fact shot Frederick Archer, and only learned of the mistake from the infallible Miss Quinton. Which in turn resulted in Miss Quinton and Nathan being shot at and Miss Quinton's son being snatched. When Alec and Nathan had rescued Samuel, they had been implicitly instructed to go to

Dover. But then Alec had run off in the middle of making love to his wife, well at least she thought it was the middle because Alec was still dressed when he decided to not finish what he had started, and then she had run after him, and she didn't really know what had occurred after that.

And now they were on a dinghy, fighting the Channel to make it to the ship that would carry them to France. Sarah tried very hard to filter the events that had occurred between her husband running off and them ending up in this dinghy. After all, when this was all over, she would go back to being the wife in a marriage that the War Office had forced. And there were some things she just did not want to remember.

Like what it was like to fall asleep in Alec's arms.

She didn't want to remember the look in his eyes when—

She dug her fingernails into her palms, hoping to draw blood. A terrific wave came over the side of the dinghy, and Alec's grip tightened. It became hard to breathe, but she didn't want him to loosen his hold on her.

A sailor behind them shouted. Sarah tried to get the water out of her eyes. The salt stung them, and more water appeared where she had just removed it. When she could finally see, the horizon had been blotted out by an enormous, black hole. But it wasn't a hole. It was the ship. Sarah clenched her teeth even as the blood rushed out of her head. Once they were on that ship, that was it. They were bound then. There was no hope of escape the moment they boarded.

A sailor was pulling her up, but Alec had not let go of her. She was torn between the two of them, but Alec won, keeping her anchored against him.

The sailor yelled in French, and Sarah only blinked at him. The water surging all around them made it impossible for her to hear him. But Alec responded. Sarah swung her head around to stare at him.

Alec spoke French?

Of course, he did. It would be ridiculous to think otherwise. He was a spy for the English in a war against the French. Of course, he spoke French. She wasn't sure why she thought she may have to translate for him. It was moments like these that made her detest his effect on her. She was a perfectly competent spy when he was not so close.

Now, Alec was pulling her toward the ship. A rope net had been flung down the side. Sarah stared at it before gazing down at her filthy, ruined dress. How was she supposed to climb that in her current state?

"I'll be right behind you," Alec shouted in her ear.

Sarah turned around and, feeling not at all like shouting, pointed at her skirts. Alec looked down at them and then back at her face, an expression crossing his features that she had not seen in quite a while.

Alec looked positively delighted.

Sarah started to raise her eyebrow, but Alec was already bending down toward the hem of her skirt. He reached between her legs and grabbed the back of the skirt, drawing it forward and dragging all the skirts up into the sack created by the back hem of her dress. He shoved the wad of fabric into her hands and smiled wickedly. The water stabbed through the sheer lace of her stockings, but the leers of all the French sailors stabbed even more sharply. She stared at her husband, her skirts in her hands and her legs bared for all the French Navy to see.

Alec could not have looked more pleased.

Fury swamped her, and her fist came up before she could stop it. Alec avoided it, and the momentum swung her completely around. She would have kept reeling right into the Channel had Alec not caught her.

"Easy, love," he said against her ear, as he placed her now uncoiled hand on the rope net. He nudged the back of her thigh with his knee. She lifted her foot, placing it on the net before she regained the sense to strike him again. So they climbed the net, Alec literally on her back, pushing her up the entire way.

And she knew she wouldn't have wanted it any other way.

They reached the deck before she wanted to, and the heat of her husband's body left much too quickly. She stood for a moment, balancing herself with the new rocking motion on this much larger vessel. She realized Alec was frowning at her, but her brain wasn't working any longer. She had been wrapped up in the man she loved for much too long, and when that happened, she turned into a complete mess. Gone was the capable and well-skilled spy for the War Office. In her place stood Sarah Beckham, orphan, incapable of almost nearly everything.

But then Alec reached over and ripped her skirts out of her grip, hastily striking the wet material back down to cover her legs. Her brain clicked back into motion as he frowned more deeply at her. This was delightful. Now he thought she wanted to show all to a bunch of randy sailors. That must be typical behavior for the daughter of a whore.

An officer approached them. At least Sarah figured it was an officer. The sailors were obviously not dressed in uniform as the ship sat in the middle of the Dover port, so she couldn't be sure. But this man walked with an elegant, pompous posture that dared anyone to question his rank.

"Bienvenue, mes amis," he said, "Or is it hello, welcome, my friends?"

His voice had an odd grating sound that tickled Sarah's ears. She wanted to reach up and scratch them.

"Hello is correct. I'm not so sure about the welcome part, and the friends part is definitely not true," Alec said, smiling through the whole statement. Sarah wanted to scratch her ears again.

"Perhaps in time," the officer said, "Allow me to introduce myself. I am Octave Teyssier. I am captain on this vessel. I have had excellent accommodations prepared for your journey to the Comte de Montmartre's chateau." Sarah again wanted to scratch her ears at the tone he used to say chateau. "I wish you no discomfort, and I assure you, you will be taken care of with our best intentions."

Sarah doubted they had the same definition of best intentions. The captain spoke with an odd cadence. Every few words were paused with a strange moment of silence as if the captain searched for the next word.

Alec nodded, ever the diplomat. "Merci, beaucoups."

"Perhaps you will join me for supper after you have had time to settle in," Teyssier gestured behind him, grandly inviting them on board. Except he was gesturing at a pair of large, scary looking men holding harpoons, so Sarah didn't feel very welcomed.

"I doubt it," Alec said without the slightest inflection to his tone.

Someone prodded Sarah in the back to get moving. She started to turn around to give a good scathing admonishment, but Alec was already moving. He grabbed whoever had done the prodding and simply threw him overboard. Sailors everywhere started to move toward Alec. Teyssier raised a hand, and all motion ceased.

"The lady is not to be touched, n'cest pas?" he asked.

Alec adjusted his jacket and nodded.

Teyssier inclined his head in acknowledgement.

It seemed words were too volatile at the moment.

Sarah stepped forward and slipped her arm through Alec's before he started their own private war on this French ship in the English Channel. After all, the odds were deplorable.

Alec slipped his hand into hers, holding her more tightly

against him, and despite how the wind bit at her skin through her tattered dress, despite the steady gazes of the menacing men with the harpoons, despite the fact that their only hope depended on an American's ability to get to the Duke of Lofton in time, despite all that, she felt safe when Alec held her hand.

The captain turned away, and Alec pulled her along after the departing man.

"Are you all right?" Alec whispered, his breath brushing against her ear.

She nodded, no longer feeling capable of speaking.

Watching the man she loved toss another overboard simply because the other had been touching her did things to her insides. Why must he always have this effect on her? Just once, she wished she would keep her composure long enough to show him just how good a spy she really was. Except it never seemed to happen.

Soon they were led below decks. The space was tight and smelled too much like feet. She caught a glimpse of the sailors' hammocks, swinging slightly with the rocking of the ship. A few of them were occupied, and the men eyed her like a Christmas Day goose. Her grip on Alec's hand tightened. His other hand came up to cover hers, smoothing away the sudden tension.

They were led down two decks, and the air grew squalid and stank. Sarah swallowed, trying to keep the bile from rising in her throat. The captain must have stopped because Alec stopped, and she nearly ran into him. She pressed tightly to her husband's back, as the passage required them to walk in a single line. She could barely see through the dimness and looked behind her as the hair on her neck suddenly stood up. There was no one there. The ship just stretched into blackness, but she still huddled closer to Alec.

Sarah tried to move her head around the small space

between Alec's shoulder and the wall of the passage. She was reminded once again of how broad his shoulders were when she tried to see the captain in front of him. Alec adjusted some, and she finally saw the captain sifting through keys on a long chain attached to his waist.

The metallic pinging ricocheted harshly down the passage. Teyssier apparently came to the one he wanted, for he stopped sifting and stuck one into a door Sarah had not realized was there. The panel was flush with the rest of the wall, and the poor lighting prevented her from seeing it.

"There you are, the best accommodations on the ship. Except for mine, of course." The captain turned so Alec and Sarah could squeeze by him in the passage, but Alec stopped moving before Sarah thought he should have. She turned about in the small room and nearly ran into the open door. She looked up, down, and side to side.

"These are the best accommodations on the ship?" she blurted out before she thought about it.

The captain shrugged his shoulders, adjusting once more so one of the frightening harpoon men could wedge into the passage in front of the door. Sarah didn't know where the man had come from and found herself unconsciously backing up into Alec.

"At least the room has a door," Teyssier said and closed that door in their faces.

The sound of the lock sliding into place might as well have been a cannon going off as the sound exemplified their current situation like nothing else could.

Sarah spun around and pushed her husband away from her. He moved maybe a couple of inches because of the space, but it was the act of pushing that Sarah needed to remove some of the emotion that was building up in her.

"You had to leave!" she spat and instantly checked herself.

There were things she did to push Alec away from her.

She yelled at him. She degraded him. She had even called him names. But there were some things that could be misconstrued as unbecoming of a lady. Behavior that was more apt to be seen on the spawn of whores. And Sarah tried hard to never exhibit such behavior. So now, she reigned in her emotions, so turbulent inside of her she doubted she could ever truly control them. And this she took as clear evidence of her origins. A lady would be naturally capable of controlling herself whereas Sarah clearly was not.

"Yes, I just had to leave," Alec said, much too weakly for her tastes.

She looked at him then, watching the shadows shift over his face, and for the first time in days, Alec looked tired. Sarah reached up and laid her hand against his face, hoping to draw some of the aching weariness out of him. Alec's eyes flared with sudden heat, and Sarah realized what she'd done. She pulled her hand away and looked for a place to hide. Which obviously there wasn't such a place, so she sat on the only bunk in the room, ducked her head, and pretended she was invisible.

Alec sat down next to her, and she noticed how he was careful not to touch her. His efforts were exaggerated by the closeness of the space. Now Sarah really wished she were invisible.

Or at least not a prostitute's accident.

If she were a real lady, there wouldn't be a problem. But she wasn't a real lady, and when people said Countess she didn't know they were speaking to her. It had been four years, and she still couldn't respond to my lady. Yet Alec had been responding to my lord his entire life.

God, why did she have to fall in love with a damn earl?

The lantern's swinging light drew her gaze, and she became fixated on it. Neither of them spoke, and she doubted Alec wanted to say anything to her. She didn't want to say anything to herself, even if she could think of something to say.

She didn't know how long she had been staring at the light when the lock suddenly turned in the door, making her jump.

Alec stood up, sloshing over the grime on the floor, and stepped in front of her, shielding her from whatever was coming in the door. But instead of Harpoon Man it was a short, stooped black man carrying a tray of food. Sarah's stomach reacted violently, growling at the sudden possibility of being filled. She covered her stomach with her hand as if that would stop the sound from emerging. Alec backed up to let the man in. The stooped man carried the tray over to the bunk and set it down next to Sarah.

Sarah smiled at him and said, "Thank you."

The man stopped and appeared startled. Sarah didn't know if her words or her nearness had upset him. But the man seemed to straighten, even though his back remained bent and his head hung at an awkward angle.

"You're welcome, my lady," he said in a gravelly voice before shuffling out.

The door slammed quickly shut behind him, the lock banging into place.

Sarah stared at the food, not sure if it was really there or not.

"Can we eat it?" she asked, not looking away from the bread, cheese and fruit.

Why she asked such a ridiculous question, she did not know. There was something about Alec's nearness that turned off the simple mechanisms in her brain that would have allowed her to function as a normal human being.

"If it's edible," Alec answered, picking up the tray to sit down on the bunk. He placed the tray on his lap and studied the food. "I've heard the fare isn't that marvelous on this vessel."

He smirked at her, and the awkwardness from the time before the door had opened suddenly disappeared.

Alec picked up the loaf of bread and ripped it apart. He raised an eyebrow at it, and Sarah laughed. She caught herself on it though, and the sound turned into a hiccup. Alec raised that eyebrow at her now, but she didn't care. She snatched a part of the bread and ripped a chunk off with her teeth. The food hit her stomach with a thud, and she felt the vibration clear to her toes.

Alec stared at her.

"What?" she asked around another mouthful of the sinfully soft bread.

Alec shook his head. "I'm just waiting to see if it's poisoned."

Sarah stopped chewing so quickly she bit her tongue. "Poisoned?" she managed around the wad of bread in her mouth.

Alec nodded, his expression grave.

Sarah swallowed, feeling the bread scrape all the way down.

"How do you feel?" Alec asked.

How did she feel? How did she feel? He had just let her poison herself, and he was asking how she felt?

"My lord, I believe I'm—"

Alec ripped off a piece of bread and popped it into his mouth. He watched her while he chewed and then swallowed hugely as if mocking her with it.

"It's good." he said, "Amazingly fresh. They must have just brought on a new load of food stuffs." He eyed the loaf of bread as if it might come alive.

Sarah hit him. She smacked his shoulder as hard as she

could, given the small space didn't allow much room to swing.

"Ow," Alec said without feeling, ripping off another piece of the bread.

"Why did you do that? Why did you make me think it was poisoned?" she asked.

Alec shrugged. "I don't know. It just popped into my head."

"Popped into your head?"

Alec shrugged. "It's not like it's actually poisoned. I really didn't think you'd believe me, and it would all just be a bit of fun to ease the..." he gestured around them, "Tension."

Sarah watched his face as his eyes settled on hers, and she felt the heat rise into her cheeks.

"How are you so sure it's not poisoned?" she asked.

"They need us alive, Sarah." His voice had lost its humorous lilt.

Of course, they needed them alive. Of course, they did.

Of course.

Alec watched her much too closely, and Sarah discovered a new interest in her hunk of bread. Alec went back to the tray of food as well, and Sarah could let her body absorb the food more easily. She chewed carefully, not rushing. She didn't want to fill herself up too quickly.

But then Alec held up a single grape between his fingers.

"Grape?" he asked playfully.

Sarah leaned forward and sucked the grape out from between his fingers.

It wasn't until she noticed the stricken look on Alec's face that she realized what she'd done. The grape seemed to lodge in her throat halfway down, and her bread became terribly interesting again.

"Sarah—" Alec began.

"May I have some cheese, please, my lord?" Sarah asked, pitching her voice at the most aristocratic tone she knew.

Alec sighed, and Sarah looked at him. His entire body had seemed to deflate with that one sigh, and Sarah's chest felt painfully constricted. What did that sigh mean? Was she even qualified to say what it meant? Wouldn't she construe it to mean what she wanted it to mean?

Would she think it meant he loved her, too, and was frustrated with all this dancing around they did when it really meant that he was tired of being married to such a nobody and couldn't wait until something could be done about it?

Sarah raised her chin higher. "Cheese, my lord?"

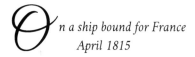

CHAPTER 2

On a ship bound for France
April 1815

SARAH CAME AWAKE SLOWLY, her muscles wakening with every breath she drew. Someone was blissfully rubbing the muscles in her back. She arched into the hand and purred.

And then her eyes flew open, and she saw...

Nothing.

Her face was pressed against her husband's shirt, and all she saw was the contorted images of buttons and pleats. She tried to drag her arms up to push him away, but he was holding her much too tightly to move.

"Easy, love," he said against her ear. "I'm tired of all your fighting."

Sarah stilled instantly.

He was tired of all the fighting? What about her? If he was tired, she was exhausted. It took all her energy to stay mad at him every hour of every day, so he wouldn't figure out how much she loved him.

So why was he tired of all the fighting?

And why the hell did her head hurt so badly?

Then she realized she was back on the bunk, intimately entwined with her husband. Every muscle in her body responded, tightening in defense.

No, no, no, no.

She didn't want to remember how this felt. She didn't want to remember how any of this felt.

"It's all right, Sarah," Alec whispered, his hand continuing its sensual stroke up and down her back. "I'm not going anywhere."

What?

What did he say?

He wasn't going anywhere?

What was he talking about?

"I don't know why you're so afraid I'm going to leave you. I'm not, Sarah. I never was, and I never will," he said, bringing her closer to him if that was possible.

Something that felt suspiciously like tears burned her eyes. That was ridiculous. She didn't cry. Of course, she didn't cry.

Of course.

But he kept talking, and he wouldn't stop, and she was afraid he was going to say the one thing she didn't want to hear, didn't want to know, because until she knew it, she could still pretend. Pretend anything.

But he did say it, and it wasn't at all what she had expected him to say.

"I've been in love with you since the first moment we met."

She burrowed her face into his chest.

The first moment they met had been a disaster.

* * *

THE FIRST MOMENT they met
  Four years, five months, eight days and some hours ago

SHE JUST WANTED to get this whole bloody thing over with.

Sarah scratched her arms under the itchy fabric of her dress. She could understand why the War Office wanted her to get married, and she could even understand why it had to be done so quickly. But really, was such a grand affair necessary?

She stood at the back of Christ Church Greyfriars, surveying the domain. Her side of the church was pitifully empty, but what had she been expecting? Her tutors were there. Her voice and piano instructor. And her governess. Five people attending one's wedding was better than no people.

However, the Earl of Stryden more than made up for the dearth of wedding guests. She wondered if they wouldn't have to pop over to St. Paul's to pack them all in. The wreath of orange blossoms on her head tilted again, and she shoved them back into place, pushing the lacy fabric of the veil off of her neck. She scratched where the material had irritated her skin.

"Excuse me," said a soft voice behind her.

Sarah whipped around, nearly sending the wreath of orange blossoms catapulting off of her head and beheld the most beautifully exquisite man she had ever laid eyes on. His visage instantly made her want to smooth her hair and check to see if the sash of her dress was straight. Her gaze traveled down the length of him and back up, seeing but not really understanding what she was seeing. She had never seen a more perfect man in her life. He was tall and broad shouldered certainly, but his blue eyes were intense and his smile only flickered on his face, begging attention in case one would miss when it would blossom into a full, all out smile. His face was all angles, shadows and light, intoxicating in their makeup. She wanted to run her fingers along his jaw line just to feel the stubble there.

"Yes?" Sarah asked, although it really didn't come out entirely. "Yes?" she tried again.

"I thought we should perhaps meet before...the, uh, the ceremony," he said, his voice smooth even with the apparent stalls in his sentence.

She could forgive him the stutters in his speech not only on account of his handsome qualities but also on account of the fact that he, too, was being forced to wed a complete stranger at a moment's notice.

"Of course," Sarah said, automatically extending her hand. "Sarah Beckham. I'm pleased to meet you, my lord."

The earl seemed to hesitate, but Sarah wasn't fully perceiving her surroundings correctly, so she brushed off the hesitation, thinking it only the tension of the moment that had also stuttered his speech.

"My lord?" he asked.

Or perhaps maybe he was just simple. In which case, Sarah would be mightily disappointed that such a visage was wasted on someone such as this.

"Yes, my lord. You are the Earl of Stryden, aren't you?" she asked.

The man hesitated again, but then that flickering smile spread into a full one, and Sarah had to gulp in breath to remain upright.

"Yes, I am the Earl of Stryden, but please, call me, Alec. I'm sure I would want you to," he said, his voice washing over her in a lovely caress.

There was something about his sentence that Sarah thought she should think odd, but his hand slipped into hers before she could fully process it. His grip was firm and gentle all at once, and her brain scrambled in her head to keep up.

"And the pleasure is all mine," he whispered, bringing her hand up to his lips.

All coherent thought fled Sarah's mind. The heat of his lips burned clear through the satin of her gloves. Her stomach clenched, and she almost swallowed her tongue when she tried to speak. Perhaps she should leave the speaking to the earl.

"I hope this hasty affair does not offend you," the earl was saying.

Sarah shook her head negatively.

"I know the War Office can be quite abrupt in their intentions."

Sarah only nodded.

"Are you sure you're all right, Miss Beckham?"

The earl's face had taken on a charming concerned expression. Sarah felt herself leaning into it, felt her head tipping back, raising her lips to just the right level to—

She straightened so abruptly the orange blossoms slid down the side of her head. She shoved them back into place and clenched her toes in her slippers in order to force herself to stay rooted in reality.

"Yes, I'm quite all right, my lord. I hope that you are all right as well. That is, I mean, I hope this arrangement doesn't displease you."

She had spoken to enough earls in the past to not start tripping up now, but then again none of those earls had been hers. Hers. Yes, it was only because the War Office had obligingly dropped him in her lap, but the fact was this beautiful specimen was soon to be hers.

The earl seemed to think on his answer longer than Sarah would have thought necessary. And it was that brief moment of hesitation that had her euphoric bubble bursting. No matter the circumstances, she was certain the earl still thought of her as only an illegitimate offspring with no title or heritage.

"Yes, the arrangement is more than agreeable," the earl finally said.

The earl was smartly dressed in solid black, which might have been odd considering the fashions of the day, but she was not one to judge how noblemen dressed. His dark hair fell over his brow in what would probably have been called a dashing manner. His skin was slightly tan, as if a hat never protected his face. There were faint wrinkles at the corners of his eyes. His nose was slightly crooked as if it had been broken once. And his expression was sheepish.

Sheepish?

"My lord—"

"Ooo, you two have met! Brilliant!"

Sarah braced herself as a woman in a magnificent red dress swooped in from the nave. It was the Duchess of Lofton, Jane Black, and the earl's stepmother if Sarah remembered correctly. The duchess was by all standards beautiful, especially considering she was on the other side of fifty. Fine lines were just starting to work their way into her features, features that were neither delicate nor strong but commandeered attention nonetheless.

Sarah nodded her head, rattling her orange blossoms. "Yes, your grace, we have met."

The earl reached out and threw an arm around the duchess, laughing rather obnoxiously.

"Oh yes, we have met, Jane. Me and Sarah, here. Me, being Alec, and her, being Sarah. You know?" the earl said.

He laughed that obnoxious laugh again, and Sarah wanted to scratch her ears. Good Lord, she hoped he didn't laugh like that all the time. She wasn't sure if she could stand it.

The duchess looked up at the earl. "What are you talking about?"

"I'm just talking about me, the good ol' Earl of Stryden."

The duchess nodded.

"Would you excuse us, please?" she said to Sarah, and Sarah automatically nodded, unsure as to what was going on.

The two walked away from her toward the hallway that led off to the stairs up to the choir loft. Their heads were together, whispers passing between them. Then the duchess let out a bright Oh, dear! and swung back around toward Sarah.

And then the duchess laughed that same, loud obnoxious laugh.

What was going on here?

"Of course, of course," the duchess said, striding back toward Sarah with her arm through the Earl of Stryden's, "Of course, you were talking about him being the earl and all that. Now, is everything all right, dear? Is there anything you would like changed?"

The duchess made a gesture, and Sarah wasn't sure if she was gesturing to the church or the world at large. Depending on the scope of the gesture, Sarah's ideas of what needed changed varied drastically.

"No, everything is lovely," Sarah said, her voice having lost its will to leave her mouth, her mind so befuddled with the tableau before her.

"Splendid," the duchess said, much too brightly for Sarah.

"Oh, yes, everything is splendid," the earl concurred.

"Everything is splendid!" the duchess said again.

Sarah moved her head back and forth between them, and then somebody slapped her back. She almost fell off her feet with the impact.

"Yes, everything is splendid!" said a loud, booming voice almost in her ear.

Sarah forced herself not to cringe and looked up to find the source of the voice. It was the Duke of Lofton, looking striking as ever and incredibly similar to his son.

"And I see you've met—"

"The Earl of Stryden," the duchess and earl said together.

Sarah was not ignorant in the matter of suspicious behaviors. She knew when something fishy was going on. In the orphanage, she had always been the first to know when they would not be getting their evening porridge. She had always warned the other children to fill up at the noon meal. Sensing something was amiss now was something even an amateur could have figured out.

But the Duke of Lofton did not hesitate a moment.

"Yes, the Earl of Stryden. My son," he said, moving to put an arm around the earl's shoulders. The earl still had his arm through the duchess's, and all three smiled so brightly it hurt Sarah's head.

"What's going on?" Sarah asked, putting her hands to her hips and smashing the small bouquet of posies she held.

"Nothing," the three said together.

Sarah looked into the church as organ music began to play. The guests grew restless in their pews, and the priest shifted from foot to foot at the altar. She looked back at the duchess, the earl, and the duke and decided she'd have to figure it all out later.

"It looks like we must get started," she said.

The three nodded together but didn't move.

"Shall we?" Sarah asked, gesturing toward the church with all the waiting people.

"Yes!" the duchess all but shouted, dragging the men with her into the church.

The three walked slowly down the aisle. Slowly. Slowly. Sarah watched them, feeling her suspicions grow. There was something going on, and she was going to find out what it was.

Sarah waited for the earl to reach the altar and the duchess and the duke to take their seats. She started down the aisle and realized quite suddenly that she was nervous. She saw the earl standing so calmly in front of all these people when her insides were dancing jigs around her skeleton. How could he be so calm? Of course, he probably had vast experience interacting with the likes of the people that were staring so scrupulously at her. She had never had that experience.

It was true that the woman who had taken her out of the orphanage in The City had been wealthy, but she had also been a recluse. Sarah had only been out in society once really, and well, that was a disaster she tried not to remember. It had been a country house party at the Duke of Kent's, and Sarah had made a complete fool of herself. Not that it really mattered. She doubted anyone remembered.

But as she drew closer to the Earl of Stryden, she was reminded of how pitifully inadequate she was to be his wife. Not only in breeding but in experience. She just hoped to God that she did not fall in love with him.

She had almost reached the steps up to the altar when the doors to the church flew open and banged loudly against the walls. The wind rushed in, forcing women to clamp onto their hats lest they fly away. A few not so quick women did manage to lose their hats and now were scrambling to get them, fearing to remain in such an impolite state for so long.

And then somebody stumbled through those doors. He was partially dressed, his collar hanging around his neck, his waistcoat open, and his breeches only half done up.

And he was singing.

"Today is the fateful day when I marry my Lady Mady! And if she says she'll be my wife, I'll love her for all my life!"

He tripped on the next down beat and rolled down part of the carpet covering the aisle. He sprang up, though, greeting people in the various pews.

"'Ello, 'ello. Look at all of ye! Kind enough to show up at...show up at..."

He spun around and sent himself careening into the opposite set of pews.

"This is my wedding, isn't it?"

His face ended up in a woman's hat that was overflowing with flowers. The man proceeded to smell everyone.

"Oh, lovely! Oh, love-lee!" he squealed and spun around once more, gaining a few steps on the aisle.

Sarah finally got a good look at his face, and once more the breath was sucked out of her. She turned around to look up at the man waiting at the altar. The earl obviously hid a laugh behind his hand. Sarah looked back at the man prancing up to the altar. They were identical. Her fists clenched, snapping the stems of the posies.

She turned back to the earl, and he caught her looking at him. He shrugged his shoulders.

"I'm Nathan Black," he said, extending his hand. "The Earl of Stryden's brother," he gulped on another laugh. "And that's the Earl of Stryden."

Sarah swung back to the other man. He had come right up to her and stopped dead. His mouth hung open, and Sarah almost fell over from the stench of alcohol. The bile rose in her throat, and her temper rose in her blood.

She opened her mouth to tell this man exactly what she thought of him, but the man beat her to it.

"It's you," he whispered and fell backwards, completely passed out with drink.

* * *

On a ship bound for France
April 1815

"At least we were actually married after that," Alec said, smoothing his hand down her back.

Sarah pushed away from him, and Alec let her go, so she could look up at him.

"After Nathan roused you from your drunken stupor," she said, her voice amazingly less forceful than he had expected.

He reached up and rubbed a smudge of dirt from her cheek. Her head tilted slightly into his palm at his touch, and he wondered if she noticed. Her eyes were much too sharp though, and he figured maybe she didn't notice because she was thinking too hard. He wondered if he could stop that and started to lean in.

"You know, I never asked you what you meant," she said before he could get his lips on hers.

"What I meant when?"

"When you said it's you."

Alec felt a trickle of wariness run down his spine. He rubbed his thumb over the skin of Sarah's cheek, having forgotten to remove his hand from her face. It seemed she had forgotten as well. Her skin was paler than he would have liked, but considering the situation, she looked pretty good. But not good enough to hear what he had to say yet. He had spent four years remembering a night from very long ago and doing all that he could to never allow Sarah to remember that night. To remember what he had done to protect her. He still could not speak of it.

"Just that it was you, the bride. I was scared to death of you."

She wrinkled her nose, making the deep lines around her mouth from the overbite wrinkle.

"You were afraid of me?"

"Why do you think I was drunk?"

"You got drunk because you were afraid of me?"

Alec felt his cheeks heating. "It was more that I was afraid to get married. I thought you were going to be a shrew or something."

"A shrew?" Sarah shrilled, sitting up.

The ceiling of the bunk was much too low, and Alec caught her before she hit her head against it. He drew her neatly down to his chest, pinning her on top of him with his arms around her waist.

"I am not a shrew," Sarah huffed, her voice much softer because he had brought her head closer to his with a hand around her neck.

He massaged the tight skin there, but the tension quickly raced back even as he rubbed it away.

"I know you're not a shrew. Now, at least. I didn't know when the War Office said I was getting married."

"You don't think I'm a shrew?" Sarah asked, barely loud enough for him to hear.

His hand stilled on her neck.

Sarah looked insecure. He had never seen her look insecure. She had always been brimming over with confidence that she threw in anyone's face who doubted her, either with a sharp retort or a fist to the gut. He'd experienced both and no longer questioned her ability to fight back even if her confidence lacked solidity. But now her eyes had gone soft, watchful, completely dependent on his response to her quiet question. And he felt a moment of panic, his resolve to say something mature finding its way to the surface.

"I don't think you're a shrew," he said, his voice equally as soft.

He thought that a safe response. Very adult of him.

"Even though I sometimes get angry with you?"

Her voice had not strengthened, and Alec felt himself stepping onto shaky ground. He had never been the dominant one in this relationship, and he wasn't sure what to do. He wanted to swallow the tension in his throat as if that would help bring the conversation to a level he knew how to handle. A level that required a joke and a laugh. He kept his arms firmly around her and told her exactly what he thought.

"Because you sometimes get angry with me."

She frowned. "What?"

"I don't think you're a shrew because you get angry with me. It takes a brave person to point out others' shortcomings in an attempt to improve the person."

She tried to roll off of him, but he tightened his arms.

"I'm not a brave person because I pick on you," she said, the rough note back in her voice.

Alec felt his heart slow down but also regretted the loss of their momentary reversal of roles.

"You don't pick on me. You try to make me a better person."

She slammed her hand against his chest, and the wind rushed out of his lungs.

"Alec, don't lie! I pick on you to make myself feel better!"

As he struggled to regain his breath, he realized her face had gone absolutely ashen. She struck again, violently trying to get away from him. He let her go, and she rolled toward the wall putting her back to him.

He tried to rise up on his elbow to look at her face over her stiff shoulder.

He raised a hand to reach out for her and said, "Sarah—"

"Don't touch me," she cut him off, her voice void of any emotion.

He looked at his hand, no longer sure what to do.

His wife had finally let him in, but now she had not

31

only thrown him out but slammed and locked the door in his face. He thought he had said all the proper and mature things the situation called for. He eased down on the bed, shifting as close as possible to her without actually touching her. The narrowness of the bunk helped in his endeavor, but she only moved farther away from him. He stopped when she was almost up against the wall.

Her stifled breath mixed with the sound of the water hitting the sides of the ship as it floundered in the Channel. And he tried again.

"Sarah, why do you have to make yourself feel better?"

She took three whole breaths, and Alec thought she wasn't going to answer. But then she did.

"Because I'm not an earl."

Her voice had returned to that insecure tone, and Alec felt his hopes rising. If she was insecure enough about something, perhaps he could get her to talk to him. He nestled closer, not actually moving closer, but in his head, he was closer to her.

"Sarah, I don't think you can ever be an earl. You're a girl," he said, feeling the return of his usual demeanor.

A sound emerged from her that resembled a laugh, but it was muffled by what sounded like a sob. Sarah was crying? Now Alec did move closer.

"Sarah? Please tell me what's wrong."

He had never asked her that question. He'd never been brave enough to. A question like that was bound to get a necessary extremity ripped off. But if he didn't ask now, he knew he would never ask.

"You deserve a lady," she whispered.

He leaned his head over her shoulder, resting it gently there so he could hear her better. She didn't recoil from the touch, and he carefully slipped an arm over her waist, not pulling her back against him, just letting it rest there so she would be physically aware of him.

"You are a lady, Sarah."

She sniffled, and he leaned in a little more, adding a little more weight to his hold on her.

"No, I'm not. I'm a...a...bastard."

Alec turned his face into her hair, which incidentally smelled horrible, but he held his breath and nuzzled into her neck, forcing her to not shrink mentally away from him.

"Nathan's the bastard, love," he said automatically and cringed when he realized he had brushed off a genuine concern of hers because he had accidentally resorted to a familial response about his brother.

But then Sarah let out a soft laugh that ended on a hiccup, and Alec felt his insides unwind.

"We're both bastards," Sarah said.

Alec shook his head, letting it fall back on her shoulder so he could see part of her face in the dim.

"Maybe technically, but Nathan really is a bastard."

Sarah turned her head and smiled briefly at him. He barely caught the sight of the tear tracks down her cheeks before she turned back to the wall.

"Ah, Sarah, I don't know why your birth matters so much. I don't care who you were. I only care about what you've become. And I love what you've become."

"You do?" Sarah whispered, not looking up at him.

"I do. Very much."

He settled back down on the bed then, pulling her against him so he cradled her in his arms. Her disgusting hair ended up his face, but he pushed it away without gagging. He was sure he smelled equally as delightful and was not going to hold it against her. He let the silence fill the berth, simply enjoying the feel of Sarah.

"Alec?" Sarah whispered after a while.

"Mmm?" he said, watching the lantern swing shadows over the ceiling of the bunk.

"It matters to other people."

Alec's resolve faltered slightly, unsure of what she was speaking. It was true there were often whispers about the previous life of the now Countess of Stryden, but Alec had simply ignored them. What society thought of his wife meant little to him. He only cared how he felt about his wife, and he was certain from the day he met her that he loved her.

"I don't care," he finally said, hoping that would end the conversation.

But something tickled at the back of his brain. For four years he had tried to get his wife to love him. He had felt her loathing for him at a deep level, an instinctual level. The same primal unease he had felt as a boy after his mother had died giving birth to him. That struggle to justify his existence because he had killed his own mother, and he had tried everything to ensure his father loved him. He was certain his father did love him now, but a part of Alec was also certain that it all depended on Alec's ability to make his father laugh. He had tried the same tactic with Sarah, but it only seemed to make her angrier, leaving him unable to talk to his own wife.

But why would Sarah care so deeply about what society thought of her as an earl's wife?

"I care. I don't want people thinking you married below your station."

Alec felt the words like a punch to his gut. He got up on his elbow and pulled her shoulder so she could see him. Her face was blotted with red, and her eyes were watery.

"You think I married below my station?"

Her sad expression turned to one of bewilderment at his words.

"If anything, I married a woman who is far too good for

34

me," he continued. "And I pray every day that she doesn't realize."

Sarah didn't say anything. Her mouth was open, but nothing came out. Alec worried that he had said too much. After all, he'd never been in a position to say what he was thinking. It was rare that Sarah didn't display her feelings with a right cross, so he had always kept his thoughts to himself. But now, Sarah merely lay beneath him, completely sapped of all signs of life. It seemed like the perfect time to bear his soul without a joke or a laugh, but whether or not Sarah believed him was apparently a different matter.

"You think I'm too good for you?" Sarah finally asked.

Alec would have thought the question a normal one from anyone other than Sarah, but when Sarah asked a question such as that, it carried with it a note of accusation, as if him thinking anything good of her carried with it a hidden dagger meant to stab her.

"Yes, I do, but I think I'm getting better and maybe one day, I'll be good enough." The last word barely came out as his throat started to close. He swallowed hoping to clear the sudden obstruction, having no idea what was happening to him. Four years was a long time to convince someone that you were worthy of their love without success.

"Alec," Sarah whined, suddenly sitting up.

She pushed against his chest to get out from under him, and his head flew up, thudding solidly against the ceiling. Sarah froze as the pain seeped sickeningly slowly through his scalp. He closed his eyes, not wanting to look at the old Sarah who had apparently returned and wanted to cause him as much bodily harm as she could.

He collapsed on the bunk and went to touch his throbbing head, but his hands collided with hers.

His eyes warily opened, fearing that he may find Sarah moving in for the kill while he was down. But instead of finding a wife bent on murder, he saw Sarah looking utterly contrite. And then her hands were slipping around his aching head, supporting his head as if that would help the pain.

"Oh, Alec, I'm sorry," she said, examining his head for what he did not know. Did she think the collision had opened the skin? Did it? He watched her face more closely to see if the situation was worse than he thought.

And why was she apologizing?

Sarah never apologized. If she was at fault, she clobbered him until he admitted it was his fault.

He liked this new Sarah. Not that he didn't like the old Sarah. Hell, the old Sarah had made him weak at the knees, but he feared this different Sarah was going to go straight for his heart. And he knew he would never be able to recover from that.

But maybe he would be able to make her laugh now. Maybe he could finally make her love him. Maybe he could push the guilt back just a little bit further as he did every day of his life.

It seemed she was done with her inspection, but she kept one hand under his head, holding it carefully while she braced herself above him with her other hand.

"Does it hurt?" she asked.

He raised an eyebrow, feeling braver with every word she spoke. "You've never asked before if it hurts," he said, feeling his heart pound with the statement.

He had never spoken so brazenly in front of his wife, and he wasn't sure what her response was going to be.

"I know," she said simply.

"You know?" he asked.

"Yes, I know I never asked if it hurt. I had meant it to hurt all those other times. I didn't have to ask if it did."

She looked him right in the eye the whole time, and Alec

felt his admiration for her growing, that seedling of hope surging with added life. He tried to pull the strings of this conversation together.

"So you wanted to hurt me, because I'm an earl and you're not, and other people would care about that difference, so by inflicting pain on me, it would make you feel better about the whole thing?"

The question made no sense to him, but Sarah responded immediately.

"Correct, my lord."

Well, at least he was correct in his nonsense.

"You really care what other people think?" he asked.

She looked down then, as if drawing more courage from the reserves deep inside her.

"I know you care," she said, looking back up at him.

"I bloody well do not!" he nearly yelled, indignantly.

Sarah's face suddenly hardened, and Alec realized he'd stepped over a boundary.

"Yes, you do. You fought in that duel right after we were married over a mistress! You do care what people think!"

She tried to get off of him and the bunk, but he clamped onto her arms.

"What the hell are you talking about? I never fought a duel for a mistress."

Sarah's eyes blazed in fury. "Don't lie to me, Alec. You may think poorly of me, but don't lie."

He shook her because he really felt like doing it just then.

"I'm not lying, Sarah, and I damn well don't think poorly of you, and I never was in a duel over a goddamn mistress!"

Sarah latched onto him, her grip just as strong as his. "It was only a few days after we were married, Alec. You left the house before dawn with Nathan, and you took the dueling pistols out of the library. I saw you."

Alec shook his throbbing head against the grubby pillow. "No, Sarah, I—"

"No, Alec, I won't listen to you if you're just going to lie to me."

Sarah suddenly let go of him and pushed against his stomach attempting to move over him to get off the bunk. Her fists in his gut jammed his internal organs into places they did not want to be, so he let go of her. After all, where the hell was she going to go anyway with the door locked and Harpoon Man on the other side?

Sarah's skirts got tangled in his legs, and she almost fell to the floor after freeing herself from his grip. He caught her and helped her upright. She brushed off his hands as if shedding lint from her garments.

"Sarah—" he started, sitting up on the bunk and consciously watching his head.

"No, Alec."

He stood up and half slid, half walked over to where Sarah was shielding herself in the corner. She was doing that thing where she pretended to be invisible, and it drove Alec insane. He grabbed a hold of her, spun her around, and shoved her up against the wall. The ship pitched, and Alec had to plant his feet to keep them upright.

Sarah looked terrified, but he had something to say and he was going to damn well say it.

"I was never in a duel over a mistress, Sarah. I was in a duel over you."

CHAPTER 3

L ondon, England
   A few days after Sarah and Alec were married

"Why are we doing this?" Nathan asked, yawning hugely.

"Because," Alec answered, closing another cabinet under the bookcases along the wall.

He knew the dueling pistols were in here somewhere. He never really occupied the library though, and he definitely never made a habit of using the dueling pistols, so he wasn't positive where the pistols were exactly.

"Because why?" Nathan asked.

Alec straightened, put his hands on his hips and turned around in a circle. He had checked all of the cabinets under the bookcases built into the walls. Maybe they were in the desk. He walked over there and shoved his brother's feet off the desk so he could get at the drawers.

"Because I said we're doing it," Alec said, pulling the drawers open down one side of the desk.

Nathan lounged back in the chair with his eyes shut. "Why do we have to do it so early?" he asked.

"Because what we're doing isn't exactly well accepted anymore, and we don't want anyone to find out," Alec mumbled, sifting through the correspondence he'd stuffed into the second drawer down. Why did he receive so much post? Who the hell wrote to him?

"Why couldn't you ask someone else to be your second? I could have slept in."

Nathan yawned again and put his feet back up on the other side of the desk, leaning back in the chair, making it squeak loudly.

"Shh," Alec hissed at him, looking up at the door to the hallway. "I don't want to wake Sarah."

"Why are we not waking Sarah?" Nathan mumbled, falling asleep in the chair.

Alec hesitated, no longer sure what he was allowed to tell his brother and what was to remain sacred to his marriage. It didn't matter to him that his was an arranged marriage that was really a fraud. He was taking this thing seriously, and by God, he was going to make it work. When he had seen his bride standing at the front of the church, he had known everything happened for a reason. If only he could make her laugh, then maybe he wouldn't have had to go to a duel at dawn.

He said to his brother, "I don't want to upset her."

"Sarah? Upset Sarah? I really don't think this would upset Sarah. In fact, I think she would very much like to be your second. Why don't I pop upstairs and ask her so I can go home to bed?"

Nathan brought his feet back down to the floor to stand up. Alec seized his shoulder and shoved him back into his seat.

"Stop being ridiculous and help me find those pistols. We're going to be late," Alec said.

Nathan raised an eyebrow. "Ridiculous?" he asked. "Out of all the Duke of Lofton's sons, I would have to argue that you have always been the ridiculous one."

Alec looked at his older brother. "The Duke of Lofton only has two sons, and ridiculousness does not appear to be working on the lady wife. So will you help me find those pistols?"

Nathan's face took on a fleeting moment of puzzlement, as if he were figuring something out, but the hesitation quickly passed.

"You know," Nathan said. "You've never been in a duel before. Why suddenly start now?"

Nathan began to open drawers on the other side of the desk.

"I have a reason to start now," Alec muttered with his head half in the third desk drawer.

He hoped his brother hadn't heard him, because he seriously did not want to broach the subject of why he was going to a dawn appointment over his wife's honor.

"You let any number of mistresses go without vengeance and yet one wife you've known for less than a week suddenly has you slapping the first cheek that dares utter a word that may be construed as insulting."

"I didn't slap his cheek with a glove."

"No, you couldn't because you punched him instead and then threw the glove onto his prone body."

Alec slammed the last drawer, which had Nathan raising an eyebrow at him.

"What happened to not waking Sarah?" Nathan asked.

"Shut up."

Alec rubbed his forehead where he felt a massive headache brewing.

"I think I've found them," Nathan said, rattling around in a drawer.

Alec looked over his brother's shoulder. "They're really wedged in here."

Nathan rattled some more, and the case suddenly popped free sending Nathan into Alec. Alec caught him and helped them both to regain their balance. Nathan set the case on the desk and opened the latches to free the lid. The two stared down at the two gleaming silver pistols with their heavy barrels, solid grips and hair triggers.

"Do you have any ammunition for these things?" Nathan asked.

And Alec felt the last of his hope die a withered death.

Minutes later the carriage rattled over the cobblestones of the path through the park.

"The second is not supposed to get the bullets for the gun," Nathan argued.

"Yes, he is," Alec grumbled in response, watching the trees slide by the window.

"No, he's not. The second plans where and when the duel is to take place. He is not responsible for artillery."

"Dueling pistols are hardly artillery."

"They're in the same family."

"And isn't that unfortunate," Alec said derisively, looking at his brother.

"Ha. Ha." Nathan matched his tone. "We could stop by Father's. I'm sure he probably has black powder and such lying around."

Alec felt like raising an eyebrow but doubted he had the strength.

"We're are not stopping by Father's on the way to a duel to ask him for ammunition for said duel. I don't think that would go over very well."

"Why not? You have always been good at making Father

laugh. Tell him a joke, and he may hand you some shot. It sounds like an excellent plan."

Alec did not bother looking at his brother. He had spoken the very truth that now plagued him. He had made his father laugh, had made him love him. But he could not make Sarah laugh.

The carriage came to a stop in the grove just off the path. The area was completely sheltered by a landscaped hedge and was a favorite for dawn appointments. Another carriage set on the other side of the grove with the Earl of Wheaton's colors on it.

Nathan eyed the carriage through the window and asked, "Do you think he'll realize there isn't a bullet in it?"

Alec did not bother to give that question an answer. He grabbed up the pistol case and alighted, Nathan right behind him. The Earl of Wheaton emerged from his carriage, striding across the grove to meet them in the middle. The earl's normally rather handsome face was purple along one side and his eye was swollen nearly shut thanks to Alec's right cross.

"Wheaton," Alec said when the man was close enough.

"Stryden." Wheaton nodded, "My second, Mr. Fletcher, perhaps you know him?" he asked gesturing behind him. "He is getting the rapiers out of the carriage. I hope you don't mind that I prefer that we use the set. I realize some men have their own rapiers, but this set was specially made for occasions such as this."

Wheaton's good eye moved back and forth as if to indicate the situation in its entirety.

Alec nodded, feeling his teeth grind.

"Of course. Would you excuse us?" he said more than asked, grabbing Nathan's arm and dragging him back toward the carriage.

"Rapiers? Rapiers?" he hissed as soon as they were out of

earshot. "Why did I spend so much time searching for these damn things?" Alec flung the pistol case back into the carriage, not caring in the least what happened to it. He slammed the carriage door shut for emphasis.

"I guess I misunderstood the arrangements," Nathan said, shrugging.

"You misunderstood the arrangements? Are there any other arrangements you might have misunderstood? Such as are you sure this is a duel to first blood or a duel to the death, because that seems like a very important arrangement not to misunderstand!" Alec accented the word by poking his brother in the chest. "You are the worst second in the history of dueling!"

Nathan stepped in front of him, blocking out the rest of the grove.

"Alec, what's wrong?" Nathan whispered.

Alec massaged his forehead. The headache was a hurricane wreaking havoc in his skull.

"I don't want to make a habit of dueling to protect my wife's honor," he whispered. "But I can't make her laugh," he said, sensing how the words did not make sense but continuing anyway. "I don't know what else to do."

"What do you mean you can't make her laugh?" Nathan asked.

Alec's memory flashed an image from a long ago time, another time when he had not made Sarah laugh. A time when things had not been as serious as they were now. But he couldn't tell Nathan about that memory. He had not even told Sarah, for he was certain if she knew, she would hate him even more than she did now.

"I just can't," Alec said. "Let's get this over with."

Alec pushed around his brother and strode back to the middle of the grove. Wheaton waited with a sword case. When Alec approached, he unlatched it and extended the case toward Alec. Alec slipped his hand around the hilt of one of the swords nestled inside and pulled it free. He stepped back, completing a few experimental thrusts with the weapon.

"Now then, this is to the death, correct?" Wheaton said, taking his sword out of the case held by Mr. Fletcher, who, unfortunately, still looked intoxicated from the night before.

Alec casually turned his head in his brother's direction feeling a murderous rage welling up inside him. Did one go straight to Hell for fratricide?

Alec turned his attention back to Wheaton. He didn't really feel like killing the man. He was an all right bloke, after all. Wheaton had been pampered a bit too much, perhaps, but he didn't drink overmuch or gamble or ruin debutantes. He just had his nose stuck too far in the air to notice the merits of anyone below eye level.

But more importantly, did Alec feel like being killed?

No, he did not.

He felt like living happily ever after with his wife. He felt like going home right now, sneaking into her room through the connecting door of their chambers, and slipping into bed beside her. He felt like waking her up with a kiss that said everything he didn't know how. If he were killed today, he would never be able to do any of those things, and that made him very, very unhappy.

But what if he did kill Wheaton?

Would that make Sarah love him? Would she want him in her life? Would she laugh?

Probably not.

If he killed Wheaton, he would probably start more whispers and that was sure to make Sarah hate him even more.

And his wife would still have no need of him. She would still look down her nose at him for being unnecessary, unneeded and unwanted. A burden the War Office made her carry.

So with a heavy heart, Alec raised his sword and fought to stay alive just so Sarah could continue to look down her nose at him.

* * *

ON A SHIP BOUND *for France*
April 1815

"BUT YOU DIDN'T KILL HIM," Sarah whispered.

Alec looked at his wife who was sitting next to him on the bunk, obviously being careful not to let any part of her touch him.

"How do you know?" he asked with a touch more accusation than he intended.

Sarah's face colored a deep shade of pink. "I followed you," she said.

Alec swallowed the instant burst of anger. "You followed me?" he whispered because he really felt like screaming.

Sarah nodded, not looking at him. "I thought maybe she would be there, and I would be able to see what she looked like."

"Who would be there?" Alec asked, even though he was pretty sure he already knew the answer.

"You know," Sarah said, shrugging one small shoulder. "Your mistress."

Alec bobbed his head more than nodded. "And why would you want to see my mistress?"

Sarah shrugged that shoulder again, and Alec wanted to touch her. He wanted to hold her in his arms, so she wouldn't feel so insecure. He didn't like her feeling insecure. She was beautiful and smart and funny and...nice. Sarah was nice. Above everything else, that was what he loved most about her. She had never really been nice to him though, but that didn't really matter. He had seen her be nice to other people, had seen her innate caring sense just seep out of her into others. Had seen the way she didn't know she did it, and how other people were affected by it. And now, he felt like giving her a little of her own caring, so she wouldn't look so sad. If he couldn't make her laugh, then maybe he could let her know he cared. Even if he wasn't sure how.

"There was no mistress," Alec whispered as Sarah continued to look so heartbreakingly miserable.

"I didn't know that."

"If there had been a mistress, why would you have wanted to see her?"

Sarah looked anywhere but at him. He raised his hand and caught her chin, turning her head toward him. She looked at him briefly and then shut her eyes.

Alec was not going to have this conversation without her looking at him. And if they couldn't talk, there was really only one other thing that he wanted to do just then.

He kissed her.

He kissed her softly, gently holding her head between his hands, so she couldn't pull away from him without ripping her ears off. She didn't respond, but he didn't know if that was because she didn't want to or because she was too scared to. He traced the line of her lips, and finally felt a tremble pass through her, but she still didn't participate in the kiss. She stayed still beneath his hands, her lips unmoving. He coaxed her lips open with pressure from his. One of her hands came up to his chest, but it didn't push him away. So he changed the angle and invaded her mouth, invaded her resolve in order to crush it. She moaned softly, and he thought she leaned into him.

But then she tore herself away from him, and he did nearly rip her ears off. She stood up ungracefully as the ship pitched beneath her, and slid over to the corner. She wrapped her arms around herself.

He hated it when she did that.

"Sarah—"

The sound of the lock scraping back had him lurching out of his seat. Sarah turned around and took one step toward the door, but he was already in front of her. He stretched out his arms to both sides, brushing the walls of their prison and effectively caging Sarah behind him.

Harpoon Man stuck his head in the door. "C'est," he began but seemed to change his mind, "There is une problem."

Sarah ducked her head under Alec's arm. "Quelle problem?"

Harpoon Man backed up a step, withdrawing his head from the crack in the doorway. He frowned at Sarah and carefully closed the door.

Sarah removed her head from under Alec's arm, and Alec heard her take a giant breath.

Alec turned and looked at her.

"What?" she said when she realized he was looking.

Alec shook his head.

"I only asked him what the problem is," she said as he continued to look at her.

She opened her mouth a third time, but he cut her off.

"Why did you want to see her, Sarah?"

Her mouth remained open and unmoving a full five seconds after he finished his question. And then she swung around to face the corner again.

So he grabbed her and spun her back around.

"Sarah, answer me." He paused, watching her nostrils flare. "Please."

Her eyes went dangerously flat after that, and her nose stopped flaring.

"I wanted to—" she began, staring hard at his chin.

He shook her a little when she stalled.

"I wanted to see what...what..." She shrugged her shoulders beneath his hands. "You know," she finished, looking down at her feet.

Alec leaned his head down, resting his forehead against hers.

"Sarah, I—" He didn't know what to say. What could he say that would convince her that it was all right to talk to him? To really talk to him? To pour out her heart to him? But what? Normally, he would have delivered an inappropriate jest just then, but Sarah didn't laugh with him.

"Sarah," he finally said, "when I was young, about eight or nine, I fell out of a tree and landed on Nathan, who was trying to catch me."

Sarah's head moved, and Alec straightened to let her look up at him.

"I squashed him, Sarah. He was unconscious for at least a minute after I landed on him. And I shook his shoulders and slapped his face, but he wouldn't wake up. I thought I'd killed him, Sarah. And I was never so scared in my life. But then he did wake up, and he called me a name, and I started to cry. And then I yelled at him for almost dying on me. By then Father and Jane had heard me screaming and had come running to see what was wrong. I had broken Nathan's arm, but he was alive, and Father carried him back to the house, and everything was fine.

"But I had nightmares for weeks after that, only in the nightmares, Nathan didn't wake up. I was afraid to sleep at night. I would lie awake and stare at Nathan's bed just to make sure he was breathing. Sometimes I would get so scared, I would go down the hall to Father and Jane's room. I never knocked though. I didn't want my father to think I was scared of something like nightmares. So I just sat on the floor and...listened...and stared at the shapes the moon made on the scary portraits that lined the hallway. "

Here at least he stopped his story long enough to roll his eyes in mock horror of the portraits at the Lofton estate. But the gesture had no effect on Sarah. No smile came to her face as he had expected it would not. Sarah just watched him, still beneath his hands. His thumbs moved against the softness of her shoulders in a sort of calming motion, and he wondered when they had started doing that.

"Father and Jane used to talk. All night sometimes. They had only been married then for about three years, and Jane...well, you know about Jane's first marriage, do you not? To the Earl of Doring?"

Sarah nodded once, but he felt her tremble beneath his hands. The Earl of Doring had abused Jane until he had suddenly dropped dead beneath a lady employed at Madame Hort's House of Leisure.

"Jane wouldn't talk to Father about her marriage to Doring at first. She wanted to keep all of those terrible things from my father. She didn't want that kind of thing to taint her new happiness. But in the end, she couldn't do it. She couldn't keep all of those things welled up inside her. She needed someone to witness it. She needed someone to know. So she started to tell my father. He knew about most of it anyway, but Jane needed to say it out loud, to have someone listen while she told her story. And I would lie by their door and fall asleep listening to their whispered voices as Jane told my father everything."

Alec stopped because he didn't know how much to say to make her understand. He had never had such a conversation in his life. She looked at him and not at his chin or his feet, so he thought maybe he'd said enough. And then Sarah opened her mouth, and he felt relief start to spread through him.

But then the door opened, and Alec was spinning around, covering Sarah with his body.

Teyssier stood in the doorway, his unusually blond hair as perfect as before, contrasting starkly with the dark stubble of his jaw.

"It seems," he said, "That the weather has worsened considerably. I fear we must remain in port until it clears." He adjusted his wrinkled jacket. "I am certain you understand."

He bent his head and withdrew.

"Alec?" Sarah whispered, sounding hideously small behind him.

"I know." Alec nodded, not turning to look at her or moving away so she could move again.

"Do you think...Thatcher..." Sarah's voice faded away as her reluctance to form the question burned in Alec's ears.

Alec did turn now and pulled Sarah roughly against him. Her arms came quickly and tightly around him, shocking the breath from him. He held onto her, rocked her in a basic gesture of comfort, comfort for him or her, he didn't know.

"Thatcher will make it, Sarah. I promise you."

* * *

DOVER, England
More than a few hours earlier

"WE ARE GOING to get bitten from that," Sarah said, wrinkling her nose and taking a step back.

Alec agreed with her, but he still felt slightly out of sorts from the shock his system had taken from the freezing ride through the English countryside. So he collapsed on the bedbug-ridden mattress in the room they'd been led to at the inn and closed his eyes. He could feel his body turn on its internal repair mechanism, and it was almost as if a charge of energy began to seep through him as his body began to regain its strength.

He felt the mattress dip as Sarah sat down beside him. He wanted to open his eyes to make sure she was where he thought she was, but he didn't have either the energy or the guts to look.

She sat right next to him.

Not on the other side of the bed. But on the side he had collapsed on. She perched on the edge with her back rubbing against his hip. He groaned and turned his head into the extremely smelly pillow.

"Alec, what's wrong? Are you getting worse?"

Sarah moved, and he thought she stood, leaning over him. He could smell her and not in a romantic, smells-like-lilacs sort of way. They had been traveling for roughly eight days without any sort of bath, and neither of them smelled like a bouquet of roses.

But the thought of Sarah leaning over him in concern seemed ridiculous to him. No matter what had happened the last time they had stopped for the day. His body stiffened as memory burned brighter. He groaned again and rolled over burying his face in the pillow, hoping bedbugs would go right for his eyeballs so that pain would block out the excruciatingly dim yet amazingly clear memory of what had occurred during that last stop.

Then Sarah grabbed his shoulder and shook with such force that he thought his eyeballs would fall out before the bedbugs could get to them.

"Alec! What is it? Please! Do not frighten me so, my lord!"

She shook him again, and the bed threatened to collapse at her onslaught.

"I'm fine," Alec murmured into the pillow.

He did not need his wife bouncing on the bed with him just then. He really did not.

Then Sarah slugged him and got off the bed. Alec felt much better.

"Where are we, do you think?"

Sarah's voice was farther away now. She had probably moved to one of the two windows he had seen before he had collapsed. The sun was just starting to rise, and a thin crack of orange spread through the drab curtains and illuminated their various holes and tears.

"Dover," he mumbled.

"Really?"

He heard the rustling of her skirts as she turned toward him.

"Yes."

"What are we going to do?"

Alec rolled over and opened his eyes but didn't even contemplate sitting up.

"Unless you have the strength to take on the two men standing outside our door, the ones with the pistols in their belts, then I think we do nothing," he said, looking up at the cobwebs spread over the ceiling.

"So we're just going to let them take us without a fight?"

"We already fought. Well, at least I fought. Feel free to engage in your own fight though. I won't stop you."

"Must you be so immature at a time like this?"

And wasn't that the truth put into words? Sarah thinking him immature when all Alec ever tried to do was to make her smile. Was to make her love him. If she thought he was being immature, she should really enjoy him when he was being downright childish.

"We should do something," Sarah whispered, but he wasn't sure she was speaking to him any longer.

Sarah moved the curtains then, letting in more of the strengthening daylight. Their captors only moved them during the night, so it had been quite a while since they had seen much of the daylight. Mostly, they had tried to sleep when they weren't being bounced around in a carriage, or for Alec, being raced through a blinding, numbingly cold rainstorm without a jacket or a hat tied to the top of the carriage. That was something he did not want to relive. Hell, he didn't want to live it the first time.

But it wasn't the cold or the stinging rain or the jarring every time the carriage had hit a rut that had tormented him. It was all the images that plagued his mind when he thought of Sarah left alone in the carriage with the oaf with the gold teeth. You can call me Sven, he had said. Alec had called him every name but Sven in those long hours on top of the carriage. Thinking on what that bastard could have been doing to his wife had stabbed deeper than any of the shafts of rain that had pierced him.

Of course, what had happened after they had untied him from the top of the carriage and hauled him into that shack where he and Sarah were to remain for the day had helped cure him of any of the lingering fear of what had happened to Sarah, but then it had made everything in general by far worse than it had previously been.

"Is that Matthew Thatcher?"

Alec was out of bed and standing at the window faster than he had ever thought he could possibly move mere seconds before. He leaned over Sarah's shoulder, unconsciously wrapping his arm around her waist to draw her to the side so he could see. He didn't notice how she stiffened at his touch.

"That is Thatcher."

Matthew Thatcher's decidedly American hat was fairly hard to miss in England, but now it was hardly perceived as Dover was a port town and saw all sorts of people. Thatcher could be any bloke off of any ship that had made port at Dover. People sifted past him on their way to the shops that were just opening. Thatcher stood almost directly across the street, his head bent as he lit a slim cigar. The light of the match cast his face in an unearthly glow.

"He doesn't smoke," Sarah said.

Alec, whose arm was still around his wife, shook his head. "It's a signal."

"A signal?"

"He's telling us he knows we're here, but he's going for help."

"Why is he going for help? There are only two of them out there!" Sarah whispered so harshly it was almost loud.

"I don't know," Alec whispered, feeling unease settle on his bones like a jacket that was tailored too snugly on one side.

Thatcher looked up, his cigar clenched between his teeth. Alec met his eyes briefly, but Thatcher was already turning away.

Sarah spun around so quickly Alec almost fell off of his feet.

"What are you thinking, Stryden?"

Sarah's eyes were squinted to an unnaturally sinister degree, and Alec backed away.

"I think this is much bigger than two men outside our door."

He stepped farther away.

"I think we've been brought here to be exchanged. Traded."

"What?" Sarah's mouth moved into a serious sneer of doubt. It was a look with which Alec was well acquainted.

"Thatcher could have taken those two men." Alec pointed at the door as if Sarah could see who was standing beyond it. "But he didn't. I think there's something much bigger and much worse than we had originally thought."

"Like what and why? Why are you so important?"

Alec frowned at her. "I know you do not think very highly of me, but in some circles, I'm quite the thing."

He sat down on the bed with greater force than he had intended, and the bed sagged precariously. Both he and Sarah stopped to watch and see if it would completely break. It didn't, so Sarah picked up the conversation.

"What I think of you is not important. Why do others think you're so important?"

"I'm a titled spy. Meaning I'm a nobleman in a dangerous, potentially treasonous position."

"Treason? How do you figure treason into this?"

"I could be bought."

"No, you couldn't," Sarah said, which had Alec looking up at her sharply. But then her face paled, and Alec knew she hadn't meant to blurt that out.

"You're right. I can't be bought, no matter the price. But they don't know that. So, I'm valuable in the right hands."

"And now, French hands want you?"

Alec stared at her as the images that question suggested floated in his head. Sarah blushed, and Alec thought he could probably savor her embarrassment, but for some reason, it tasted sour. So he continued on in a rush to let her awkwardly worded question slip by unnoticed.

"Yes, but for what is the real question. And why go through all this trouble to get me to Dover?"

"There can't be anything going on in Dover. This place is filled with agents. Your father said so."

"He did?" Alec asked.

Sarah nodded. "The morning you left I went to his house

to look for you. At breakfast, he said nothing could be going on in Dover because there were so many agents here."

Alec felt a familiar dislike grip his stomach. "I'm glad to hear that my sudden departure did not cause you such anxiety as to upset your appetite."

Sarah opened her mouth, but her eyes darted quickly to the side. Alec felt the hairs on the back on of his neck rise. Sarah was hiding something.

"My appetite is not the point, my lord," Sarah said to the wall behind him. "Why is Dover important? Why did they bring you here?"

The door swung open then, and Sven walked in carrying a basket covered in a dirt smudged cloth. He flashed his gold teeth.

"To trade the earl, of course," Sven said, answering Sarah's question.

Alec had the sudden urge to say I told you so to Sarah, but he thought she would find such a gesture immature as well. So he settled for crossing his arms over his chest in victory.

"You see, my lady, I'm being paid a handsome sum to bring his lordship to the docks tonight." Sven set the basket on the one chair in the room that was nailed to the wall because it was missing a leg. "Please enjoy your breakfast. You will not be eating again for some time, I'm afraid." He shrugged as if the gesture would make everything better. "I just haven't the quid to waste on you lot." He adjusted his overly large coat, adding another smudge of grease across its lapels if that was even possible. He ran his hands over his hair, smoothing it down from the receding hairline.

He smiled, flashing his gold teeth once more. "Cheers, mates," he said, and then he left.

"Who would pay money for you?" Sarah asked, her tone leaving no question as to what she thought of such an impossibility.

Alec felt his momentary victory crash into oblivion as the reminder of a much bigger defeat swamped him.

The door swung back open suddenly, and Sven poked his head inside.

"That would be the Comte de Montmartre. He's going to keep you hostage, so more spies will come to rescue you. And then he'll just keep adding to his collection until he breaks the English spy network or is given an obscene amount of money for your release. It really is quite the scheme. I wish I would have thought of it." He made that shrugging gesture and slipped back through the door, closing it behind him.

"Well, I guess that explains everything," Alec muttered.

"Bloody hell," Sarah said.

CHAPTER 4

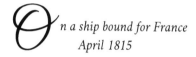*n a ship bound for France*
April 1815

"So you don't really prefer brunettes?"

"Where the hell did you hear that?" Alec nearly squeaked.

He lay on the bunk, his hands crossed over his stomach, Sarah lying in the exact same position beside him.

Alec felt Sarah's shrug against his shoulder.

"It's a rumor that I heard."

"From where?"

"Everywhere, really. I mean, it's common knowledge that the Earl of Stryden likes brunettes."

"I do not like brunettes. Who started that rumor?"

"You did," Sarah mumbled.

"How? When? What are you talking about?"

"Lady Cavanaugh. Countess Delinger. The Duchess of Creedin."

"All right, you can stop now. And I may have shown some interest, but I did not demonstrate a preference."

"You had lengthy affairs with all three of them."

"I did not!" Alec really did squeak now, and he bit his tongue as punishment. Earls did not squeak.

Sarah's head turned toward him, and her hair brushed the side of his face.

"You did, too. You even got Lady Cavanaugh with child. It's rather unfortunate that she miscarried. I'm very sorry about that."

Alec sat up to lean over Sarah. "I did what?"

"Lady Cavanaugh. Your affair resulted in a child."

"It did, did it? What else did I do?"

"You attempted to steal away the countess to Gretna Green for a quick marriage, but she objected on the grounds that she wanted her mother at the ceremony. And the duchess, well," Sarah turned pink.

"What the hell did I do with the duchess?" Alec asked between clenched teeth.

"I think it would be easier to say what you didn't do with the duchess."

"What?"

"She likes to...speak on the subject of your..." Sarah's eyes moved over his shoulder, "sexual prowess."

"I never laid a finger on the Duchess of Creedin. How can she speak of my—" His throat abruptly closed as Sarah's eyes made their way back to his. He suddenly couldn't talk about his sexual prowess to a woman he had only recently thoroughly enjoyed for the first time. "Speak of my...you know."

He lay back down, keeping his eyes on the ceiling above the bunk.

"You really never touched her?" Sarah asked softly.

Alec shook his head. "No, I never touched her. And I never tried to take Countess Delinger anywhere, let alone Gretna Green. And Lady Cavanaugh was my...partner, I guess you would say, before the War Office had me marry you. We never did anything that would cause her to become pregnant."

Sarah turned her head, making her hair crackle. "You mean all of those stories were made up?"

"Yes, that's exactly what I mean."

"And you don't prefer brunettes?"

"I prefer you, if that matters at all."

"Oh," Sarah said but didn't elaborate.

Alec felt his frustrations take on a whole new level, and he wasn't at all certain that that was a good thing.

"But what about...well...that one time...when..." Sarah said.

Alec turned his head to stare at her. She was blinking profusely at the boards of the ceiling.

"What one time?" Alec asked very softly, suddenly aware that they were having a pivotal conversation, one that could result in Sarah taking a swing at him, one that could result in Sarah never believing him when he said he loved her.

One that would result in Sarah never laughing with him.

"It was a few months after we were married. Lady Cavanaugh and you were...in the library."

"Whose library?"

As soon as the words had left his mouth he realized his mistake and could have gratefully bitten off his own tongue not to continue in this conversation. But Sarah stared at him now, her eyes suspiciously moist. Oh God, don't let her start crying. He would be doomed if she started crying.

"There was more than one library?"

Alec turned onto his side, laying one arm across Sarah, not quite tucking her against him, but also not letting her move away from him.

"There were various libraries, but they were not in the way I think you mean."

"The one at the MacDonalds' country party in Stirling. That library."

Alec felt the muscles along his spine quiver.

"Yes, that library. Will you believe me if I tell you about that library?"

Sarah nodded, and her hair crackled some more. Alec reached up and brushed it away from her face, carefully tucking it behind her ear.

"Okay, love. I believe it was raining that night."

The MacDonalds' manor house just outside of Stirling, Scotland
    A few months after they were married

ALEC CLAPPED his hand over her mouth as the thunder shook the house down to its foundations. The jagged paths of lightning continued to flash as their brilliance etched patterns in his eyeballs. The storm must be directly on top of them for the lightning to be followed so closely by the thunder.

Lady Cavanaugh shook in his arms. Luckily his hand had been quick enough, and he had caught her scream before it had ricocheted down the hall to the salon where the other guests of the MacDonalds' country party were being force to endure a musicale by the tone deaf Beverly Cousins.

He slowly moved his hand away from Lady Cavanaugh's mouth now and pushed her down the hallway toward what he hoped was the library. He counted the doors and stopped so abruptly at the fifth one down that Lady Cavanaugh nearly fell over.

"Why must I do this? Why couldn't you have asked your wife?" she whispered fiercely at him.

Alec tried the knob and found it turned easily in his hand. He would remember to thank his brother later for his excellent talent with locks.

"Because my wife hasn't the experience at this yet. She's only been at it a few months."

A sharp gasp from somewhere behind them sounded like a firework going off in a church service. Alec spun around, Lady Cavanaugh doing the same and almost sending both of them falling.

A young woman in a pale pink gown stood a few feet away from them, lightning playing across her horror stricken features. Her little pink mouth formed an "O" of surprise, and the sausage curls framing her delicate, child-like face trembled.

Alec still had his hands on Lady Cavanaugh's shoulders, so he pulled her against him and ground his mouth down on hers. Her lips tasted like sawdust, and he suddenly very much wanted to see Sarah. So he ended the kiss more forcefully than he intended, but he doubted their youthful watcher would notice the awkwardness.

"Perhaps, you can be next, my lady." Alec grinned and winked at the girl while giving a most gracious bow in her direction.

The young woman grabbed her chest and leaned heavily against the wall, seeming to have lost all support in her legs.

Alec pulled Lady Cavanaugh into the library, just barely keeping himself from slamming the door on their innocent intruder. He leaned back against the hard wooden panels instead of bashing his fists into them. Tales of his haltingly dreadful kiss in the hallway were going to be created, edited, modified, exaggerated and twisted so that by the time they reached Sarah they were going to have Lady Cavanaugh half naked in the hallway with his trousers undone and nearly to his knees. Hell, he may even have the lady up against the wall ready to—

Alec propelled himself away from the door, no longer

interested in wallowing in the self-pity created from all of the horrible stories he knew his wife was bound to hear.

"That was really rather clever of you, Alec, but your wife—"

"I know," he cut her off.

"She's very new at this," Lady Cavanaugh persisted, "And she may not be as adept at keeping up appearances if she is suddenly confronted with rumors of this incident."

Alec paused to look at her. He had not been thinking of it along those lines. He had only worried that Sarah may think he did not, in fact, love the woman he was married to.

"I will be sure to educate her on the matter," he said, forcing away the thought of embracing another woman and having to explain such a thing to his wife.

Alec moved toward the large windows behind the only desk in the oddly small library. Alec had expected the library to be larger in a house such as this. A manor house should have an extensive library, he thought, but since Alec really never spent time in any library, including his own, he really didn't know if his thoughts were accurate at all.

Lightning flashed in the windows, and Alec looked at Lady Cavanaugh. She held up her hands and shook her head, sending her dark hair swinging.

"I've got it together now, Stryden. I promise not to embarrass myself at the boom of thunder." Her bright golden eyes flashed in the darkness, and Alec felt moderately better about having kissed a woman who was not his wife. After all, he had only kissed Lady Cavanaugh. And how many times had he done that before? Surely, by now the kisses were meaningless. Hell, all kisses seemed to have become meaningless. The only ones that mattered never happened and never appeared to might happen in the near future.

Bloody hell, there was that self-pity again.

Alec pulled open the first drawer of the desk with enough

force to dislodge it. Lady Cavanaugh didn't say a word about it but started sorting through the stacks of books on the various odd tables scattered throughout the room. The light from the furious storm cast enough of a glow to make their search easier. They wouldn't risk a candle. Someone may stumble upon the library and see the strip of light under the door. Then where would they be? Kissing again, probably, and Alec did not feel like kissing Lady Cavanaugh again all too soon.

"Do we know what the map may look like?" Lady Cavanaugh whispered.

"Not really. There are some theories that it may be the Irish coastline that we're looking for. But really, it's anybody's bet."

"I don't see someone like the MacDonald betraying England."

"Odds are he's not," Alec mumbled with his head under the desk, tapping the sides for hollow spots that might be hidden compartments.

"He's not?"

Alec pulled his head out from under the desk. "We think he's being conned by the Campbells."

"Dirty bastards. Why are they conning him?"

"They need his shipping business as a cover," Alec said, turning around to the cabinets below the looming windows.

"How are they using it as a cover?"

"The Campbells tell MacDonald that they can smuggle in fine French brandy if MacDonald will allow them the use of his docks, so the ships won't look suspicious. MacDonald doesn't know that the Campbells are smuggling arms out of England on the ships, arms intended for Napoleon."

"And MacDonald is thinking he's just getting some good booze?"

Alec turned around and smiled sarcastically. "Exactly."

"Treason seems a pretty high price to pay for a fine French stupor."

"Especially when it's unknown and unintended treason."

Thunder vibrated the windowpanes above Alec's bent head, but when the panes settled back into their places, he became aware of another sound. Footsteps. Coming down the hallway. Lady Cavanaugh apparently heard it too because she was scurrying her way through the maze of odd tables to Alec. He shut the cabinet he had been poking around in and turned just as Lady Cavanaugh reached him. He lifted her up on the desk and stepped between her legs, bringing her softly against him. She wrapped her legs around his waist and put her mouth to his throat.

Alec felt the bile rise in his throat, and he swallowed it down, savoring the sour taste it left as punishment. Lady Cavanaugh was too big, too solid, too not Sarah. She didn't fit right against him. Her thick hair was full of static and crackled against his chin. Alec closed his eyes and pictured someone else, someone smaller, lighter, blonder, to keep his stomach from emptying itself.

The footsteps stopped in front of the door. Alec opened his eyes just as the knob began to turn. He bent his head into the crook of Lady Cavanaugh's neck but kept his eyes up toward the door. The tinkling of feminine giggling came through the crack before one dark head popped through followed by the little blonde head of the young woman they had encountered before entering the library. Alec heard the dark headed one's exclamation of surprise as if she were standing right next to him. Her startled Oh sounded genuine as if she really didn't expect to find what she saw behind the door.

Alec groaned and buried his head in Lady Cavanaugh's shoulder.

This caused a twitter to ripple through both girls, and the door shut with a snap.

Alec jumped away from Lady Cavanaugh as if he had suddenly learned she carried the Bubonic plague. Her expression was one of wry understanding.

"I'm sorry. I just...love my wife," Alec said as the air rushed out of his chest.

Lady Cavanaugh nodded. "I know. So does the rest of the ton," she said as her mouth twisted into a smile that revealed her straight white teeth.

Alec took a step back and came up against the cabinets behind him. "They do?" His voice sounded horribly unsettled to his ears.

"Of course, they do. It seems the only one who doesn't know is your wife. And why is that?" Lady Cavanaugh tilted her head. The lightning flashed across her face, highlighting her slightly squat nose and too rounded cheeks.

Alec perched himself on the cabinets. "I can't make her laugh," he said.

Lady Cavanaugh tilted her head. "I beg your pardon? I don't see how your ability at humor is a problem here."

Alec shook his head. "She seems to have an issue with me being an earl, but I don't understand what it means."

"Mmm. She's an orphan, correct?"

"Yes." Alec ran his fingers through his hair thinking it may relieve some of the ache that was suddenly beating the back of his forehead.

"Not everyone is comfortable in money and nobility. Especially those who have never had it. They may come to despise it."

Alec nodded. "Sarah definitely despises it. But I'm not sure it's the money she has a problem with. I think it's just me."

"How do you figure?"

Alec laughed hesitantly. "I don't think I'm what she wants."

"The Earl of Stryden is something a warm blooded woman doesn't want?"

"Not this woman."

Lady Cavanaugh slid off the desk and adjusted her skirts. She came up to him and raised one hand to rest it against his cheek. Thunder rattled the windowpanes as Alec looked into her startling golden eyes. Lady Cavanaugh was tall for a woman. Nearly six feet, and her eyes were level with his as he sat on the cabinet.

"I think you should check again, Alec." She dropped her hand and made her way back through the maze of books. "And in the meantime, I think it best that people believe your brother tried to ravish me tonight. No one is going to believe that you tried." She smiled softly, a world of empathy in the curve of her lips.

Alec nodded.

Lady Cavanaugh slipped through the doors as lightning lit up the room.

* * *

On a ship bound for France
  April 1815

SARAH PICKED her head up from Alec's chest.

"That's really what you did with Lady Cavanaugh?"

"That's really what we did."

Sarah laid her head back down.

"How did she know?" she whispered.

"Mmm?" Alec murmured.

"How did she know that it wasn't you that was the

problem?"

Alec stilled. "What do you mean?"

Sarah did not answer right away. Alec would have normally prodded her into talking with some childish remark, but there was something about the moment that made him refrain. Something made him hold himself in check, and he felt the unwanted weight of self-control.

Finally, Sarah spoke, shrugging her shoulders against his arm. "I'm not sure how to say it. To say how I felt that day. There was a lot going on in my head. It was not as if I was only marrying a person I had never met before, but I was also voluntarily joining a profession in which I could very well end up dead."

A small twinge of guilt tripped across his spine, but he did not say anything. He waited for her to continue.

"It was all a bit much, and I will admit that perhaps I acted rather out of character."

Now Alec laughed. "It was not out of character, love, but it certainly was rather impolite. You yelled. In God's church."

He felt her try to shake her head against his chest.

"It was not as if anyone in that church had never heard a woman yell before."

Alec had to agree with her on that, but—

"They may have heard yelling from a woman, but it was not expected of a lady."

He felt it the instant she withdrew at his words. She didn't physically move away, but she did not need to. He felt it in the way her breath paused ever so slightly, and she adjusted her head just the barest of spaces. And he knew that he had said the wrong thing. He should have known his attempts to make her laugh would fail once again. It was not as if this situation were any different. It did not matter if their lives were in peril as they bobbed in the English Channel aboard a vessel bound to take them to their doom. She was still Sarah. And Sarah disliked him. Intensely.

But Alec would not give up. He had made his father love him even when he had committed the ultimate sin. He had made his father love him by making him laugh. He knew he could do the same with Sarah. He knew he could, because he must. He could not imagine living the entirety of his life at odds with her.

He needed her goodness. He needed her light. He needed her tenacity. He needed her.

"Sarah?" he asked, even though there was no one else in the room to whom he could be speaking.

She responded with a quiet, "Hmm?"

"What did you mean when you said it was not that I was the problem?"

Perhaps it was dangerous, or even foolish, to resurface such a delicate topic when he had so recently upset her, but there was something in the statement that did not sound quite right to him. It settled uneasily on him as if Sarah spoke only half-truths until she could figure out the whole lie.

Now she did move away from him, and he let her. She took a deep breath, and he felt the exhale on his cheek. He turned his head to look at her lying next to him, her lovely face so close to his on the pillow.

He wanted to kiss her. He wanted to do more than kiss her. He wanted...to not be here. For certain, he wished to be with her, Sarah, but he wished it were somewhere else. Anywhere else. Somewhere warm and safe and...happy.

"Sarah?" he prompted.

"I don't know what it was, Alec," she nearly whispered, and Alec felt the prick of another half-truth.

He doubted Sarah was lying to him, but he also knew that she was not speaking the entire truth to him. It was as if she knew what she meant, but she did not wish to tell him. He wondered what it was and more importantly, why she felt she could not tell him. He wanted her to tell him everything. He had hoped that by confiding in her about his dependence on his father's voice as a little boy would help her to trust him. To bring her closer to him. But he could see his story, his sharing, had not had the desired effect. She still closed herself off to him. She stayed back and away, physically, emotionally and mentally.

"What was your favorite thing to do as a child?" he suddenly asked, not liking how it felt to feel Sarah drifting further away from him. He wanted to change the subject. He wanted to see if talking of nothing got her to speak about something.

Sarah looked at him, her eyes deep pools in the lantern light. "I beg your pardon?" she asked.

Alec shifted onto his side, coming up on one elbow. "As a child. What was your favorite thing to do?"

Sarah blinked, and then she said, "Eat."

A laugh slipped from Alec's mouth before he realized she was serious. "I'm sorry," he said quickly before she could retreat. "I didn't realize—"

"It's quite all right, my lord," she said, and he thought she would berate him, but her expression was one of mocking cynicism. "Not all of us are born to the life of leisure young Master Black had as a child. Some of us 'ad to earn our keep," she finished in an unrefined accent.

And then she smiled.

And Alec nearly died.

He would have found it humorous seeing as how he had survived up until now only to have his wife's playful smile slay him in the end. He recovered quickly though, not wanting to lose this mood. Not wanting to lose Sarah.

"Well, I beg your pardon, miss," he said with equally as drawn out polished tones. "I did not realize the caliber of the present company. I do hope you can find it in yourself to forgive me."

Sarah frowned. "Why should I forgive you? It would do no good. You would still be the same arrogant, immature earl I have had the unfortunate circumstance to be wed to for the past four years."

Now he frowned. "Unfortunate circumstance?"

Sarah rolled her eyes at him. "We were forced to wed, Alec. What part of that circumstance seems all right to you? Surely, you have not enjoyed being wedded to a shrew like me."

Alec took offense at that. "How do you know how I feel? And I believe we have already concluded that I do not think you a shrew."

Sarah blinked at him, her eyes vacant as if she were absorbing everything and letting nothing back out in return.

"What was your favorite thing to do as a child?" she asked, avoiding his question.

Alec lay back down, taking the opportunity to move just a little bit closer to Sarah.

"My favorite thing to do as a child was to follow Nathan around," he said, referring to his older brother.

Sarah did not say anything right away, and when she did, she was hesitant.

"What was it like?" she asked. "Growing up with Nathan being a..."

"Bastard?" Alec supplied, turning his head on the pillow.

Sarah looked at him and nodded. "Yes, a...bastard."

Alec shrugged. "I don't know. Nathan was just Nathan. It was not as if I knew the difference when I was eight and just wanted him to teach me how to catch trout from the streams."

Alec looked back at the ceiling, casting his memory back on his boyhood.

"Nathan had always been there. There was never a time when I didn't have a big brother, so I never really thought about him as being anything other than that. My big brother." He scratched the back of his neck where the rough fabric of the pillow irritated his skin. "But I suppose it was rather odd that Nathan could not go to things that I could."

"Things?"

Alec shrugged. "You know, like picnics and races and country parties, and—" He stopped so abruptly he nearly swallowed his tongue. He looked at Sarah from the corner of his eye, but she seemed to be merely looking at the same boards he had been. "You know, things such as that."

Sarah nodded but did not offer further input. Alec nudged her with his elbow.

"What about you? How did you survive the dodgy halls of St. Mary's? I've heard a thing or two about the young Sarah Beckham. Care to share a tale or three with me?"

Sarah looked at him briefly before returning her gaze to the ceiling. "No, I would not," she said flatly.

Alec was not deterred.

"All right, how about I share one then? As you so graciously shared the tales you had heard of me, it would be remiss of me as a gentleman not to reciprocate."

Sarah swung her gaze back him. "Whatever do you mean?"

"Did you really release a flock of hens into the nuns' cloister during prayer?"

Sarah sat up nearly hitting her head on the ceiling. She turned to him, her nostrils flaring. "Who told you that?" she asked, her voice even and strong.

Alec smiled. "It's classified. And how about the poor priest? What was his name? Something saintly like Timothy James or James Timothy or some such thing. Did you cut off the back side of his robes while he delivered the homily at mass one day?"

Sarah's mouth dropped open.

"I wouldn't have suspected you of wanting to see a clergyman's freckled white arse, but there are things about each of us that the other never really expects, true?"

Sarah's mouth snapped shut. "It wasn't freckled," she said and lay back against the bunk.

Alec smiled at the ceiling and put his arm behind his head. It was at that precise moment that the boat took a sudden dip, and Sarah rolled against him. He moved quickly, capturing her back in his arms. She did not fight him, and it surprised him. She simply lay against him, her head resuming its place on his chest.

Alec's hand traced lazy circles on her back, enjoying the feeling of warmth that spread from her body into his fingertips. They were silent then, and Alec felt Sarah breathe in and out. It was possibly the most comforting sensation Alec knew. His hand moved against her back before settling along the curve of her hip. He held it there, feeling the draw of her breath.

"Alec?" she asked, and he thought of how fragile her voice sounded.

"Hmm?" he said in response.

"I didn't—" she said but then stopped.

Alec looked down at her in time to see her nervously lick her lips.

"I didn't," she continued, "I did not do what I did that day because I thought you were dying."

She swallowed, and he felt the movement against his chest. He knew she was speaking about the hut, but he didn't want to press her.

"I beg your pardon?"

"I mean," there was more nervous lip licking, "I did think

you were dying and I thought if I...you know...you would warm up and not...die."

Alec didn't say anything. Could not say anything. His hand slid up her back, cupped the back of her head, and drew her back so that she could see his face.

"What do you mean you didn't do what you did because I was dying?"

Sarah's expression was unreadable. If there was one thing about his wife that made her a good spy, it was her incredible ability to become a blank slate at a moment's notice. And now she used that ability to keep her husband at bay. To keep Alec out. He did not like it. He prodded incessantly.

"What do you mean, Sarah? What do you mean you did it? It was me who—"

She cut him off. "No, it was me, Alec. I started it."

He blinked, feeling a sudden rush of anger well up inside of him.

"You started it? You made me believe for two days that I had taken advantage of my wife when you were the one who had started it?"

Sarah pulled back, trying to free herself from his grasp, but he would not let her go.

"I'm beginning to realize we have a problem when it comes to understanding each other, my lady. Now would you care to elaborate on that statement?"

He saw the flash in her eyes that told him she was trying to figure a way out of it. She was trying to find a way to not tell him the truth. And suddenly, he wanted to know the truth very much.

"Sarah," he said.

"Well..." she began.

CHAPTER 5

*S*omewhere in a hut in Southern England, probably on a
road to Dover
Two days ago

THE THUD of Alec's body hitting the dirt floor made Sarah
cringe. She stumbled more than ran to where he had landed
and fell on her knees beside him.

"Alec? Alec? Oh, please God, say something. Alec?" She
picked up his head and cradled it in her lap. His hair was
soaked, and his lips were a cruel shade of blue. Her stomach
rolled at the sight, and the room began to spin, but she
gripped her courage and turned back toward the door.

"A fire, please, I beg you. He's too cold. He might die.
Please." She was begging for the first time in her life, but she
didn't care. Alec couldn't die on her. He couldn't leave her.

Sven with the gold teeth smiled harshly. "I'm afraid there
will be no fire. The smoke may draw a crowd. And we
wouldn't want that, would we?"

Sarah couldn't answer him. Her tongue was suddenly too

large for her mouth and air wouldn't go down her throat to her lungs.

"Besides, the ride on top of the carriage was a punishment for causing a stir in our pleasant journey. I will not be giving comforts to him now after he has betrayed my trust." Sven put his hand to his chest and bent in a mocking bow. "I will leave one of the horses in here with ye. 'Haps the animal's body heat will help."

Sven walked out of the hut into the still pounding rain. Sarah shivered at the sound of it seeping through the deteriorating thatched roof. She turned back to Alec, but he was no more awake now than two minutes before. She stroked her hands across his cheeks hoping to draw blood to the surface to heat his skin. But his lips. His lips were terribly blue. She rubbed her fingers across them, but they were still that cruel blue when her fingers moved away.

A horse neighed in her ear, and Sarah jumped almost dropping Alec's head back on the floor. She looked up as a horse nose nudged her head. She scooted away from the animal, dragging Alec with her. The horse was amplified in the small space, and Sarah felt her courage wavering. She pushed Alec a little farther away from the horse and gently placed his head on the floor. She looked up at the ceiling as more rain fell. Nothing dripped above Alec's head, so Sarah stood up, maneuvered around the horse, and stood in front of the open door.

Sven stood in the rain with the other three men that were their captors. Sarah had seen none of their faces except Sven's, and they all wore identical dark greatcoats. The rain ran off their coats in rivers, and their wide-brimmed hats threw off waterfalls.

"Excuse me," Sarah yelled through the noise of the downpour that had been raging all night, the long night that had seen Alec strapped to the roof of the carriage, the long night that had seen Sarah nearly shredding her gloves in anxiety. Alec had been tied to the goddamn roof and all because he'd knocked Sven into the wall with a well-placed fist to the face when Sven had said something less than complimentary about her.

And now was not the time to think about what that had meant. Alec, her sudden knight in shining armor like something from a fairy tale. Orphans did not believe in fairy tales.

"Excuse me!" Sarah shouted, sounding hysterical even to her own ears.

Sven turned around.

"The earl isn't waking up."

Sven nodded once and turned back around.

Sarah marched out into the rain, grabbed Sven and swung him around.

"He is not waking up, you bastard!" Sarah grabbed handfuls of Sven's greatcoat and shook him, venting all the anger that was welling up inside of her.

Someone grabbed her from behind and flung her down into the deepening mud. Her face landed in an inch of water, and she gagged as mud went in her mouth and up her nose. She coughed hard as someone else hauled her to her feet. They started dragging her before she could get her feet under her to walk. They threw her into the door of the hut, and she bounced, colliding with the unnerved horse.

"'Haps if you give him some attention, he will wake up in good time," Sven said, snapping the door shut in her face.

Sarah stood for a moment, feeling the rain running off her body. She watched the light flicker through the holes in the door as the men moved around outside. The horse nudged her back. She swung around, sending droplets of water flying off her skirts. She pushed the horse out of her way.

"Oh, calm down, you silly animal." Sarah patted his nose and scooted around him.

Alec lay on the ground where she had left him. His lips were still that cruel blue, but his chest rose and fell in steady breaths. She stood above him and wrung her hands. She stopped when she realized her gloves were missing. Her hands were freezing, red and raw. She looked down at Alec. His skin wasn't red. Just cold and lifeless.

Sarah dropped to her knees again. Her hands fluttered once helplessly in the air above Alec's chest before they dropped. Her fingers crawled over the fabric of his shirt, unconsciously finding the buttons. She slipped one from its hole, then another and another. She watched her fingers go beneath the shirt. The shocking coldness of his skin made her jerk when her fingers made contact with his chest.

'Haps if you give him some attention.

Sarah drew her hand back.

"Alec?" she whispered and then wondered why she'd whispered.

She brushed his dripping hair off his forehead, but the lock fell back into place.

And then Sarah leaned over and put her lips to his. Softly, at first. Why softly, she did not know. But there was something about Alec unconscious that made him seem so vulnerable that it scared her. So she was gentle, but the feel of Alec's lips reminded her of another kiss, a harder kiss, a kiss of frustrated love and relieved fear. And then she was kissing him more deeply, willing him to respond as she increased the pressure on his mouth.

But he didn't respond.

So she hit him. Hard. On the chest. The thud of her fist slamming into him echoed through the thatched hut.

"Goddamn you! Wake up!"

She was crying. When had she started crying? Why couldn't she stop?

"Alec?" She kissed him. "Alec?" She kissed him again. "Please, God, Alec, wake up!"

She stood and started ripping at her sodden dress. Body heat. Her body heat would warm him. The wet material wouldn't cooperate, and her body heaved with wracking sobs. She heard something rip, and the dress finally fell to the ground. She fought with her chemise as she knelt, straddling Alec's hips. With the chemise free, she started on Alec's shirt. Her cold fingers moved quickly over the tiny buttons, startling her in their dexterity. Finally, the material fell to either side, and she could spread her hands across the broad expense of his chest, her fingers curling in the fine dusting of dark hair.

"Alec? Alec? Can you hear me?" She leaned down and kissed him again, harder, longer kisses. "Alec, please wake up."

She scooted back and went to work on his trousers. The wet material wouldn't budge, and she couldn't lift him to work the stubborn garment down his legs. So she scooted back up and fell down on his chest, her bare breasts crushing against him as she landed on her elbows. She took his head between her hands and bruised her lips as she kissed him yet again. She thought she felt a flicker of movement in him, but she cried so hard and kissed him so hard, she wasn't sure who was moving and who wasn't.

"Alec, Alec, Alec," she murmured against his mouth. "Alec, I need you."

Alec's hand at the back of her head made her jump, but his grip tightened and held her mouth against his. His other arm moved around, pinning her solidly against him. Her hips ground against him as she struggled to free herself from his embrace. She hadn't thought about him waking up and seeing her like she was, and she was suddenly terrified, vulnerable, insecure.

But now Alec had taken over. He had gone from unconscious to fully awake apparently from just her kiss. She wondered at the power she held, but she thought of all the rumors, the stories, and knew it wasn't her that held the power. It was her sex that held the power, and Sarah had nothing to do with that. She was just another woman. Any woman could have woken Alec.

But not every woman would respond the way Sarah responded. Attempting to escape, to get away from him, to not feel so frightened that he was going to realize whom he was kissing so passionately and then stop. But he had kissed her like this once before. He had kissed her with abandon, had taken her to heights she didn't know existed.

And then he had left.

A scream started in her throat, and she wrenched away from him. But Alec rolled, keeping his arms around her as he tucked her beneath him. His mouth assailed hers, and it kept her from withdrawing from the moment. It kept her from blocking out what was happening, from feeling what was happening.

From feeling that her blood was heating, racing. That her skin was far from cold, and she thought she may even burst into flames at any moment. The feel of his callused hands moving up the sides of her body, over her stomach, around to her back, brushing the undersides of her breasts, but never quite touching where she wanted to be touched.

Her legs came up, wrapping around his hips. Her back arched as his hands skimmed her breast again, but his fingers wouldn't come any closer to the spot that ached for his touch. She clawed at his back and pushed on his shoulder as if to steer him.

"Easy, love," he whispered in her ear, "easy."

She did scream then, but it came out choked as his palm finally closed over her nipple, and delicious pain spiked through her. She thought she heard him laugh, but he was doing things to her neck and nipple and her— Oh, God, she didn't know what was going on.

She pulled her arms back and shoved against his chest. He didn't move. He laughed again and bit down gently on her earlobe. She jerked as her stomach muscles clenched.

And then she realized he was warm. He was more than warm. He was sweating, his chest heaving as he drew in deep breaths of air. She moved her hands, and they slipped across the sweat slicked, tight muscles of his stomach. Her hands slipped lower than she intended and ended up fumbling with the loosened fastenings of his trousers. She didn't hear Alec's sharp intake of breath, because her fingers had found...him.

And he was much too big.

Huge, really.

And now she was truly frightened.

She had thought the stories she heard had been exaggerated or at least touched up a bit. But if anything, the stories hadn't even come close to the truth. And Sarah was worried he was not going to fit.

"Alec." She sucked in air as she pushed at his shoulders.

"Shhh, it's all right, Sarah." Alec nuzzled her ear, and she felt his hands moving where hers had just been. She bucked against him to throw him off, but Alec pressed against her, stilling her. Alec's mouth was on hers again, and she couldn't form a protest. Hell, she couldn't even form a thought as his tongue invaded her mouth. But his mouth tore away much too soon, and the protest that left her lips was not the one she had previously thought to say.

"Alec, please don't stop."

The breathy, fragile quality of her voice reinforced her fear, but she tightened her legs around him. She wanted this, she wanted this so much. And if Alec were thinking clearly, when Alec was thinking clearly, he wouldn't touch her like this, he wouldn't kiss her like this, he wouldn't make her feel like this. This was her one chance, and she was going to take, take as much as possible and give him her whole heart, because he already held it in his hands. She wasn't going to take it back now. She couldn't take it back now.

But when Alec entered her, the pleasure that had been all consuming moments before was suddenly gone as if someone had thrown a bucket of water on her.

Alec groaned and buried his head into the side of her neck.

"God, Sarah, I need you," he whispered fiercely.

Sarah bit her lower lip and tilted her hips to bring him more fully into her. She felt filled, full, and shadows of pain twitched where her muscles had clenched before. But Alec needed her, so she held on as he pounded into her, she held on as tears seeped from her closed eyes. She didn't feel the hard ground digging into her back. She didn't feel the cold drafts passing over her exposed skin through the holes in the hut.

There was only Alec, and right now, she thought, that for him, there may be only her. And more tears seeped from her eyes.

Alec stiffened and collapsed on top of her. Sarah turned her head away from him when she couldn't stop the tears. She tasted the blood as her teeth split her lower lip.

But she held onto Alec as his heartbeat slowed, as his muscles relaxed, as she whispered, "I need you, too."

* * *

SOMEWHERE, *he wasn't really sure and didn't really care*
    A few days ago or something

. . .

THERE WAS dirt in his mouth, along with a sizable chunk of Sarah's hair. But he didn't move his head. He didn't even think about moving his head. Too many things, too many thoughts, too many feelings, too many emotions coursed through his body for him to think about ordering his muscles to move his head off the ground. That was asking far too much of his muddled brain at the moment.

He had just made love to his wife.

Sarah.

He had just made love to Sarah.

And he really couldn't remember it.

He remembered being strapped to the top of the carriage. He remembered going along with it because he was terrified they would hurt Sarah if he didn't comply. He remembered the rain, how it pierced his clothing as if he weren't wearing anything at all, how he had been numb within minutes, how he hadn't felt the bumps, hadn't felt how they tore his muscles in directions they did not want to go, after the first three or four.

He had watched the rain fall. He had kept his eyes open as the drops pelted him. He had been thinking. Thinking about what was going on in the carriage below him. Thinking about what he was going to do when they released him. Which man he was going to kill first. If he was going to simply kill them. Killing them seemed too easy. He wanted them to suffer. Thinking of ways to make them suffer had kept his eyes open for hours.

And he had been listening. Listening for any sounds from the carriage below. He had thought it likely that he could break his bonds if he had heard one noise from Sarah. Just one noise and he would have shredded the ropes that bound him, taken out the driver, and commandeered the carriage.

But Sarah hadn't made any noises. In fact, he had suspected he heard a laugh a time or too. So he hadn't shredded his bindings in pure rage and taken over the carriage. He needed to see where they were taking them, who was behind this and stop whoever that was.

So he had lain in the rain, his muscles pulling, straining, as the carriage raced through the dark. He had frozen in layers. First his skin had seemed to disappear. Then his blood must have chilled because the iciness was spreading in waves through his body, transferring from organ to organ. Then the cold had struck his bones, and the iciness spread in tremors, chills that wracked his body, made him buck against his restraints, pulling his muscles when the movement of the carriage demanded that he push.

And then blackness.

His brain knew he had had too much even if he didn't know and had turned off. Only to turn on abruptly, suddenly alert and reeling to catch up with what was happening to his body, when his wife had herself pressed totally against him, her soft mouth on his numb lips.

But his body was way ahead of his brain and had simply reacted to the taste of Sarah on his lips, reacted to her warm body pressed to his cold flesh. And he had surged up toward that warmness, to that tart taste of her mouth. And when she had tried to pull away, his hand had caught her head and held her in place, desperate to keep her from leaving him.

What had she been saying right before he had grabbed her?

God, he wished he could remember. But he didn't. He only remembered her wrenching away from him, remembered following the movement of her body by rolling with her, covering her body with his so the contact wouldn't be severed. He had thought she had made some noise, but it was such a muddled blur in his head, he really had no idea.

And then she had wrapped her legs around his hips.

That he remembered. He remembered that quite well. How could he have forgotten? The woman he had loved for four years, the woman who had done everything except promulgate her hatred for him from the steps of Parliament, was beneath him and wrapping her legs around his hips, grasping at his shoulders, his neck, as if she wanted everything that he was giving her, wanted it so much that clinging to him was the only way to make sure she got enough.

He had said something then. Probably something flip. God, he hoped it was something flip, even if it wouldn't make Sarah laugh. But then Sarah had choked on a scream so he either had done something right and she liked it, or what he had said had really made her mad. He hoped it was the first and not the latter.

It was at that point that he realized her breasts were in his hands. Her uncovered breasts. He had laughed. He really didn't know any other response. His brain was thawing and with each movement of his hands, he was becoming more and more aware of just how naked his wife was. So he had laughed some more. Laughed at the irony. It was finally possible for him to show his wife exactly how he felt in the way he touched her, the way he caressed her, the way he kissed her. But the only thing his poor head was capable of doing was responding to the physical nature of the situation he found himself in.

The woman he loved wanted him.

That was all that was running through his mind, and he couldn't summon the energy to think of what to do to show her that he wanted her back. He simply reacted.

That was when she touched him.

The pleasure was so intense it was painful. Her soft palm cradled him, skimmed along the length of him. The breath rushed out of him, and the only thought left in his head was how the hell his trousers had become undone and how did he thank God that they were undone.

After that, all he remembered was pleasure.

And that's why he had dirt in his mouth and didn't care.

And if he lifted his head, he would have to look at Sarah. He would have to see reality in her face, and the harshness of that reality would gouge out his eyeballs when Sarah spoke and undoubtedly released her eternal wrath on him.

So he left his head on the ground.

Until he heard it.

Until he heard the twist in it as she tried to muffle the sound.

Until he felt the unmistakable catch in Sarah's body beneath his.

She was crying.

He was out of her and off of her in an instant. But he didn't look at her. He looked at the fastenings of his trousers as he scrambled to get them done up. He shoved at his shirt to get it tucked back in. The blood roared in his ears, and he didn't know whether or not to be grateful that he couldn't hear her, couldn't know if she was still crying.

His trousers were fastened faster than he would have liked them to be and then he didn't have anything more to look at or do. So slowly, reluctantly he raised his eyes.

Oh. God.

His wife was beautiful.

Through the gloomy, watery light that leaked into the hut through the single, muddy windowpanes along the front wall he took in the sight of her spread before him. Her skin was pale and smooth, and his fingers itched to touch. Her full breasts, her slightly rounded stomach, the curve of her shoulders. He wanted to run his fingers over all of it. Hell, he wanted to run his mouth over all of it.

And then one of those delicate shoulders shook with a sob, and Alec forced his eyes higher.

His stomach dropped.

A layer of mud caked her neck and one cheek. More mud soaked the part of her hair that rested against the mud caked cheek. She had her eyelids shut so tightly it made his head hurt. And blood oozed from her lower lip. Alec's heart sped up, and he thought he was going to be sick. He swallowed hard and drew deep breaths. But a single thought kept ricocheting around in his head.

He had just taken advantage of his wife.

He reached for her before the thought could truly solidify, before it became something that he'd actually done. He gathered her in his arms, and she didn't even fight him. If she had resisted even a little bit, he would have felt a whole lot better about it. But she didn't fight, she didn't tense, she didn't even squirm. She fell against him, lifeless. Alec felt his own tears coming on and swallowed harder.

He rubbed her shoulders and noticed for the first time that her skin was rough with cold. God, what was he thinking? She was naked and caked with mud, which meant at some point she had been wet, so really she was naked and wet and he was being such an arse by kneeling there staring at her breasts.

That thought bounced around again in his head.

He had forced himself on his wife.

But he shoved it away and rubbed Sarah's skin harder.

He could feel her tears now, hot against his neck. Neither of them had spoken, and Alec suspected neither of them would. Sarah would be too stubborn to admit she was even involved in this whole thing. She would sink into herself and pretend that she didn't exist. And Alec, well, hell, he was scared to death of Sarah, so there was no way he was going to say something. And even if he did, he knew it would not be enough.

He had forced himself on his wife.

God, why couldn't he remember what had happened? Sarah had been kissing him. He knew Sarah had been kissing him. But how had Sarah gotten naked? Had he gotten her naked? Had he made her get naked? Oh, God, what if he had forced her to touch him? He recalled that moment clearly, and he had thought she had done that willingly, but what if he had made her do it?

The tears fell from his eyes now, and he didn't dare reach up to stop them. He was afraid to stop rubbing Sarah's skin in an attempt to bring heat to her flesh. He was afraid that if he stopped she would freeze and shatter, if he stopped she would disappear.

But he had to get her dressed.

He eased her away from him, but she didn't try to raise her head. The tears fell harder now as he looked at her. He knew she was still crying, her shoulders shaking. He knew she was trying to pretend she wasn't in this moment, and Alec knew there was nothing he could do about it.

He looked around the room. Her dress was on the ground a few inches away, and he lunged for it. The material was slightly damp, but it was better than having her shiver naked against him. He pulled the dress over the ground, and the material fanned out. The collar was ripped, and buttons were missing.

Whatever Alec had eaten came up into his mouth then. He swallowed it, welcoming the acid burn, the bitter taste as the contents of his stomach went back down. Oh God, he had ripped her dress off. Had she been crying then? Had she tried to stop him? Dammit, why couldn't he remember?

He somehow managed to get the dress over her head. She moved her arms, slipping into the sleeves when appropriate, but she didn't move more than she had to and she never looked up at him. It was best, he told himself. He probably wouldn't like to look at him after the fact either, after he had forcefully taken her virginity.

Oh, God, her innocence. He knew Sarah had come to the marriage a virgin. It had been in her file. Everything had been in her file. And he had just—

He buttoned the few buttons that still clung to the soiled material, and a horse whinnied in his ear. He looked up startled, ready to defend Sarah against whatever it was. A horse's nose batted his ear, and Alec leaned back to look up at the animal. He had to wipe his eyes first as his vision was blurred with tears. But yes, there was a horse in this hut with them. How the hell had he missed that?

Alec threw himself back, his head striking the ground with enough force to make his ears ring. But Sarah landed softly over him, draped across his chest, her head resting below his chin. He held her there, keeping her face down, so she wouldn't have to look at him, wouldn't have to know that she wasn't alone.

And then he closed his eyes and hoped oblivion would come quickly.

* * *

In a hut in southern England
A few moments later

SARAH WAITED until Alec's breathing had evened out before she dared to wipe the tears out of her eyes. She tried to open her eyes, but she just didn't have the strength.

Alec was alive.

Alive.

And he had just made love to her.

More tears suddenly surged behind her eyes, but she bit the inside of her cheek, confusing her system and forcing the tears to retreat.

The echo of his heartbeat was soothing below her ear. Her fingers twitched in the dirt as she ached to wrap her arms around him. But she had already felt too much, and she didn't want to remember what that was that she had felt.

Cherished.

That was the word for it.

The way he had cradled her against him when he had become fully aware of what was going on. After the surge of desire, after the fog of unconsciousness had lifted, he had held her like she was the most important thing in the world to him. And all she could do was cry. Some wife she was. Alec probably thought he had done everything wrong, and that was why she was crying. But knowing the way she always belittled him, always put him down so he wouldn't suspect that she loved him, she couldn't blame him for believing what he did.

But she could blame herself.

She tried to keep sleep at bay, because if she slept, it would mean that at some point she would have to wake. And waking in Alec's arms was not something she wanted to experience, to know what it felt like to wake up and instantly know that you were safe and loved.

Loved.

She didn't want to know what that felt like, because you couldn't miss something you'd never felt.

But Alec's heartbeat was too comforting, his arms too secure.

Sleep came even though she begged it not to.

CHAPTER 6

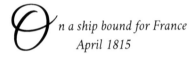 *n a ship bound for France*
April 1815

"I DIDN'T HURT YOU," Alec whispered.

Sarah picked up her head. "I can't believe you thought you did. I mean, I—" How did one address seduction with the one who had been seduced? "I forced myself on you."

Alec wasn't looking at her. He studied the boards behind her head, so she rested her head on a fist and waited for him to say something.

It was a novel idea really. She had never waited to hear what he had to say. She had always jumped into the silence with some remark meant to hurt him before he could say anything to the contrary. So now she waited as she tried very hard to believe that he may care for her.

"Did you try anything else to wake me up before you," he made a clearing noise in his throat, "forced yourself on me?"

Sarah tilted her head on her fist and looked at the same boards Alec found so interesting.

"Actually, no, I don't think I did." She turned back to look at him and found him watching her. "I said your name a few times, but—"

This was the moment when she was sure he would make her feel awkward just for the fun of it. He would say something smart about her having only one thing on her mind. He would say something immature and cruel, and she would feel as little as she imagined herself to be. But Alec didn't say anything. And for the barest of moments Sarah believed that maybe Alec at least respected her.

"I guess I thought that that was the best way to wake you up," she finished.

She held her breath. She knew she held her breath, but this was the first time that they had every spoken this freely to one another without one attacking and the other attempting to simply defend himself. So she held her breath, fearing that this equalization of their relationship might disappear or worse, implode on them. She was not sure what had overcome Alec, but since their abduction, something in him had changed. His jests were not so quick, and his smart remarks, although still present, did not hold the sting they once did. And with their demise, hope began to pool in Sarah's chest. Hope that maybe an earl could love an orphan.

But even as the thought formed in her mind, she remembered that day four years ago when all of society had watched with trepidation as she, the offspring of a streetwalker, had dared to wed an earl of the realm in Greyfriars. She had never felt more on display in her life, and Alec's performance as he had entered the church did not aid in her feelings of unease.

Sarah tried to pull her mind back, reign in her ricocheting thoughts. Right now, Alec held her tenderly against his chest, held her in his arms, cradling her as if she were precious cargo. Cradling her as if he truly cared. She held her breath, not wanting this moment to slip past her.

But then Alec smiled softly, and she could breathe again.

"It woke me up, so I guess it was the best," Alec said, his green eyes on her in the dimness.

Sarah put her head back down on Alec's chest as the ship seemed to rock more than it had been a few moments before. But as she lay there, she realized she had not answered his question fully. She had not told him why Lady Cavanaugh had been right that day when she had said no woman could resist the Earl of Stryden. And although she wanted to lay there, seeping in the warmth of Alec's embrace, she knew she owed him an answer. So she pulled away, slowly and carefully, so as not to startle Alec, and lay back against the bunk, folding her arms over her stomach.

"What is it, love?" Alec whispered to her, his breath warm against her ear as he shifted against her.

"Alec, I need to say something," she said.

The languid joy of only a breath before melted away, leaving her nerves rattled and tense, waiting for Alec's response even before she had spoken the words that needed to be said.

"Lady Cavanaugh was right," she blurted, "I do want you. I've always wanted you. Well, perhaps not at the moment when collapsed from too much drink, but very nearly right after that, but I couldn't tell you that because you were earl, are an earl, you are an earl, and I am orphan, an illegitimate bastard of the lowest class, and orphans do not marry earls, and this should not be happening right now, well, we should not be captives of the French navy, but we should also not be lying here like this—" she moved her hand between them as if to encompass the situation in its entirety, "—it just isn't acceptable, and so I decided from the moment I first realized that I wanted you that I would not want, and I would make certain that you never realized that I did want you because this—" again she moved her hand between them, "—should never happen."

She stopped, her lungs running out of air completely. Her eyes did not move from the boards above her head. Alec's breath was steady against her ear, but she dared not look at him. She had spoken the words she had been holding close to her heart for more than four years. She could not look at him now. She doubted she could ever look at him again. But she waited in silence, hoping he would not say something smart and hurtful. Hoping he would be mature enough to disregard what she had said without belittling her.

His hand came up, brushing along her jaw to cup the side of her cheek. Gentle pressure drew her face towards his on the pillow beside her. She thought about closing her eyes. She thought about not looking at him. She thought about a lot of things in the split second it took for him to draw her face towards his. But she did nothing but look at him in the dim light. And she thought of nothing. The sight of him beside her, a look of pure wonderment on his face. Her breath held in her chest again.

"I think I understood most of that monologue, but you'll have to forgive me if I must ask you to repeat things. I am, after all, merely an earl, and you must forgive me."

His tone was light and playful, but his words were sincere. In a flash of realization, Sarah knew he was trying to comfort her. Sarah knew that he understood how difficult it was for her to speak the words she had just said aloud. It was the first time Sarah had ever felt that Alec truly understood her.

"But I think what you just said is entirely rubbish," he continued, and the air swept from Sarah's lungs. "You are clearly mistaken if you think an orphan is unsuitable for marriage to an earl. As our marriage demonstrates quite nicely, an earl can marry whomever he wants. Even if the War Office demands it." He paused, and Sarah knew he was thinking. "Actually, I think it would be especially if the War Office demands it."

He paused again, pulling her closer against him with the arm that suddenly became draped across her middle. She allowed herself to be dragged into his warmth, no longer afraid that it would be the only and last time she would feel his nearness. That this would be the only and last time she would feel that he cared for her.

"Sarah," he began, and she heard the change in his tone as if it were a brass quartet announcing the arrival of a princess to a ball. "I cannot understand your perspective on our marriage, and I am afraid I may never be able to. I've lived a sheltered life. A privileged life. And it has prevented me from seeing the divides in society with such clarity as you are able to. So I ask you to forgive my limitations, and I ask that you help me to see things the way you do. I know I may have failed to do so in the past, and I know that I do not always meet your expectations of a husband, but I am willing to learn. If you'll help me."

Sarah had been able to follow him until that last bit. What did he mean when he said he did not always meet her expectations of a husband? She was not aware she had any expectations for a husband.

But it was the first bit that she clung to. His honesty rocked her. She had never expected such words from an earl, and she especially did not expect them of Alec. A pointed insult, a derogatory remark or simply a smart retort would have suited him more. But again, there was something about him here on the ship. There was something about him that seemed older.

"What expectations have you not met?" she asked, not

truly believing that she had been brave enough to ask the question.

She grew suddenly afraid that once asked, he would articulate her fears in a manner she could not control. He would realize that the expectations she set, whatever they happened to be, were not realistic of an earl. And she would lose him again. Assuming she had ever had him. Which she was not entirely sure she did.

Alec's hand caressed her cheek, his fingers sliding into her hair, massaging the back of her neck. She knew he did not realize he was doing it, but she felt the primal urge to move her head into the cradle of his palm. To press against his fingertips and feel him against her.

"I don't know what your expectations are," he said. "I think that is why I fail to meet them. I don't know what it is you want from me, Sarah."

She looked into his eyes then, saw the unfathomable depths of green. But she saw more than that. She saw the little boy who believed he had killed his brother when he fell on him. She saw the little boy who had crept down a darkened hallway to hear his father's voice to keep the nightmares away. She saw the man who had tossed a sailor of the French navy overboard because he dared to touch her. She saw the man who had done everything in his power to make her laugh.

Now she moved her hand, cradling his face in her palm. "I don't think I have any expectations, Alec," she said, her voice barely above a whisper.

And Alec smiled into the darkness. "You may not realize you have expectations, Sarah, but you most certainly do."

She wanted to respond with an accusation of innocence, but there was nothing left in her for such a fight. So she simply said, "Oh?"

Alec nodded, the stubble of his beard scraping the sensitive skin at her wrist. She shivered in his arms, and Alec pulled her closer. They faced each other now, Alec's arms securely around her. She looked up to see his face, to watch his eyes, and the nearness made her heart race.

And then his lips found hers, and all conscious thought fled. There was only Alec. There in the small space of their prison. There was only her husband. Her husband who did not push her away when she had told him she wanted him. Her husband who did not berate her for such lofty expectations. Her husband who so clearly wanted her, too.

She let his mouth plunder hers, not wanting to engage lest she do something to make him stop. She was still a novice at this, and she did not trust herself to do the right thing. But then his fingers moved along her back, and she felt her dress loosen.

"Alec, what are you doing?" Sarah asked.

"Nothing."

"Alec, you're unbuttoning my dress."

"Am I?"

"Yes, you are."

"I'm sorry. I didn't realize. Would you like me to stop?"

Cool air rushed along her skin as her dressed parted along her back. And then Alec ran one finger down the length of her spine, her completely bared spine as they had left her chemise on the dirt floor of that hut, and she tried very hard not to quiver at his touch. Something began to build inside of her, and she tried desperately to squash it down.

"Y-Yes," Sarah stuttered.

"Excuse me? What was that, my lady?"

His finger reached the sensitive curve above her buttocks, and Sarah jerked against him, unable to control her response to him.

"Alec, someone might come in," she finally managed to get out, and then she wished she hadn't.

His hand froze before it dipped lower to cup her buttocks and pull her more firmly against him.

"I suppose you're right," he said but didn't remove his hand from the inside of her dress.

And then Sarah sighed. She was not sure what had brought on the sentiment inside of her, but there was something about having her husband's hand cradling her bottom that made her feel as if everything would turn out all right in the end.

"Alec? Do you think we can rest for a while?" Sarah whispered.

Alec swallowed. She felt the movement against her forehead as her head had come to rest once more along the top of his chest.

"Yes, Sarah, I think we can rest for a while," he said.

His voice was deep and comforting against her ear, and she shivered again for entirely different reasons. She allowed herself to snuggle even closer to him as his grip on her tightened. And this time when sleep came, she let it, because more than anything, she wanted to know what it felt like to wake in her husband's arms.

* * *

UNBEKNOWNST *to our hero and heroine in the port of Dover*
  At the same moment

"LADY CAVANAUGH? LADY CAVANAUGH?"

Matthew Thatcher cleared his throat, his eyes dodging from side to side as if seeking someone to verify his current situation. He didn't do much work for the War Office of the

British empire, but he was learning that when he did, the work came with a certain degree of oddity. Whomever had thought the British were a prim and proper sort clearly never did work for the War Office. His present predicament an example of his point.

"Yes," she whispered to him, her own unusually golden eyes flashing in the muted light of the tavern.

He studied her face for longer than was polite, but he couldn't help but follow the delicate line of her nose to the soft curve of her full cheeks and the decadent line of her lush mouth.

"Lady Cavanaugh," he repeated, sounding monotonous to his own ears.

He simply could not believe that this voluptuous woman was a spy for the War Office. He quite simply had expected, well, less really. She was tall, and her long neck held her head high with a kind of regal poise. Thatcher had never thought much on a woman's posture, but there was something about Lady Katharine Cavanaugh that demanded one take note.

"Yes, I am Lady Cavanaugh," she said, "You are Matthew Thatcher, correct? I mean, I was just assuming with that hat and those boots that—"

"Yes," he cleared his throat again, "Yes, I'm Thatcher, but —" his voice stuttered in his throat, and he had to clear it a third time. "It was just that I was expecting a lady, ma'am, not a—" He stopped, not knowing the word.

"I believe the correct term is bar wench. Or ale wife if you prefer," Lady Cavanaugh said.

She winked at him, and the motion drew his attention once more to the color of her remarkable eyes. He was unsure of their true color in the haze of the barroom, but the gold flakes in them danced every time she turned her head. She turned her head away for a moment, and again, the gold flashed in the light.

"And why are we playing at bar wench?" he asked, still thinking about the color of her eyes.

"The War Office told me to," she whispered, turning her head back and threading her fingers through his hair, sliding her hands down to his shoulders so she could pull herself more tightly against him. She was practically in his lap already on the rickety bench in the corner of the tavern. He wondered for a moment how close she planned to get.

"The War Office sent you to Dover to play the role of bar wench? Why?"

"Because I'm the best actress they have. Lofton told the office that we needed people in servants' roles down here, so they contacted me and sent me down immediately."

"The office thought it appropriate to send an unmarried lady to a port full of sailors to play a bar wench?"

"Well, I am a widow. That was how I was able to play the Earl of Stryden's mistress for so long." She smiled and tilted her head just the barest of degrees to the right.

Cute, Thatcher thought. She was beautiful and cute.

She turned her head away for a moment and then back. "I think that's them," she whispered to him.

Thatcher knew what she was talking about. Honestly, he did. But could anyone blame him if he was a little distracted? Lady Cavanaugh-lady, Christ-had quite a substantial bosom, and that bosom was currently substantially bared and pressed against his ribs. So substantially, he had a right to be distracted.

Yes, his friends' lives were in danger. Yes, they were probably currently being handed over to the French where they were to be held as prisoners or maybe just killed. Who knew with the unpredictable French?

But right now a fine English lady pressed her bosom against him and ran her long fingers through his hair.

So he was going to let himself be distracted, damn it.

Lady Cavanaugh had her head turned again, watching three men on the other side of the room. The one had two gold teeth that flashed in the weak light whenever he opened his mouth.

But Thatcher studied her hair. It looked dark brown, maybe black, but he couldn't really tell in the light. He suspected it may even have lighter strands running through it, but again, he couldn't be sure.

And then Lady Cavanaugh's head swung around again, almost knocking him in the chin.

"They're looking!" she hissed, right before her mouth connected with his.

Oh, sweet, sweet Lord.

Lady Cavanaugh could kiss.

Her mouth was wide, full, and her lips soft. She angled her head in just such a way as to draw his lower lip into her mouth. She suckled, and his hands became enmeshed in the fabric at her back, pulling her more firmly against him. She changed the angle, and he swore he heard a moan come from her, but there was a strange roaring in his ears, and he couldn't be sure. Now her tongue was in his mouth, her grip on his shoulders strong as if he was her only root to earth, as if he was the only thing keeping her from floating away.

And just as suddenly as she came, she went, pushing herself off of him with a loud smack as their lips separated.

Her eyes were glassy and huge. He couldn't tell if they were frightened by what had just happened in that kiss or just startled. He really didn't know how he felt about it himself. After all, what was one supposed to think when an English lady masquerading as a bar wench thoroughly, completely, and devastatingly kissed one in a smoky tavern in Dover?

He didn't have one goddamn clue.

But across the room, he saw the three men they had been

watching move. They rose, pulling money from their pockets and dropping it on the table.

"They're moving," Thatcher whispered, thinking any speech at the moment may shatter the English lady into a thousand little pieces.

But to his surprise, she just grinned.

"Do we get to follow them?" she whispered back.

Thatcher could only nod, grab Lady Cavanaugh's hand, and start his way through the crowd toward their fleeing prey. When they reached the door, the cold air hit him like a slap, and he sucked in a breath. Even for April on the coast, it was cold. A storm brewed on the horizon, and the water in the port stirred restlessly, knocking boats into docks, and sending dockhands scurrying to secure the lines before the storm reached port. He quickly scanned the crowds of sailors moving from one drinking spot to the next until he found the three gentlemen he wanted.

"When do you think they made the trade?" Lady Cavanaugh whispered behind him.

He turned briefly and belatedly realized she was without coat in her ridiculous garb of bar wench. She must be freezing, and he started to remove his own coat. She smacked his hand.

"Do not get chivalrous on me now, Yankee. We have a mission to complete. We need to know who those men gave Sarah and Alec to, and we need to know now. Start walking."

She poked him in the back, and he did as she demanded.

"How far are we to follow them?" Thatcher asked, his path through the crowds carefully selected to avoid detection.

Lady Cavanaugh followed beside him, her own step calculated, and Thatcher made note to compliment her on it later.

"Until the very end, I'm afraid," she said.

"What if they board a ship?" he asked.

"Then we board it with them."

Thatcher stopped and turned to her. "We could end up on the Continent if we follow them on board a ship."

Lady Cavanaugh stopped as well. "Then we pretend we're an Italian lord and lady until we can be rescued. The War Office wants to know what allegiance these men have."

Thatcher turned and began following the men again, wondering what an Italian lord was like.

* * *

Also unbeknownst to our hero and heroine in the port of Dover
  Also at the same moment

NATHAN GRABBED the back of his wife's coat before she could move out of arm's reach. He snapped her back toward him.

"Where do you think you're going?" he muttered in her ear.

Nora's eyes flashed in the dim light of the alley, barely visible underneath the floppy hat he'd stuck on her head to hide her identity.

"I'm going to save my family if it's all the same to you," she whispered, her tone firm but not accusing.

Nathan grinned. "And are you going to do that all by yourself, my lady?"

Nora grinned back, her white teeth flashing in the darkness. "If you continue to be so slow, perhaps, I shall, my lord."

Nathan stopped grinning and started pulling on his wife's arm as they made their way through the rest of the alley.

They came out of the small space just yards from the docks. They were on the backside of the thoroughfare, and Nathan could hear the boisterous voices of dockhands and sailors looking for a place to lay their head that night along with a woman as company. This part of the port was seedy at best and repugnant at worst. He felt a twinge of guilt for bringing his new wife here in the middle of a cold spring night, but she had insisted. And if there was one thing Nathan was learning, it was to never tell Nora no if she said she was going to do something. No matter what that something entailed.

"Do you think they're still in port?" Nora whispered.

Nathan shook his head, the cold air sweeping in from off the water, sending a chill along his neck and down his great-coat. He pulled Nora closer.

"Thatcher has firm intelligence that they were already traded over to the French. They are now following the men who traded him. We need to see if this was a one-time event or if they are going to take more Englishmen."

Nora turned to him. "They?"

Nathan looked down at her, pausing for a moment to admire the shape of her face in the glow of moon. "Lady Cavanaugh. I'm not sure you've had the pleasure of meeting her."

Nora's head tilted. "I cannot say I have. She sounds lovely though," she finished and turned back toward the thorough-fare with its constant stream of rowdy seamen.

Nathan waited patiently even as the cold air began to rattle his teeth. He looked out to the water, at the outlines of ships bobbing in the quiet ocean and saw the clouds in the distance moving closer. Soon they would lose the moonlight. The water in the port already kicked up fierce waves, and the port was filled with the sound of ships hitting against piers and each other. But the sailors in port took no heed. The ships were safely anchored for the night. They had more interesting pursuits to tend to.

"It's that one there," Nathan said, pointing discreetly to a dock nearly ten yards down the wharf from their hiding spot.

He could not be sure if Nora looked where he pointed or simply took his word for it.

"That is where they will meet us?" she asked.

"That is where the ship is docked. The one we are going to use to find Alec and Sarah."

Nora turned her face up to him. "And we are certain they are still in the port. They must have been traded quite some time ago. Would they not have gotten underway for France? It seems dangerous to linger."

Nathan now pointed to the clouds he had spotted earlier, dark masses encroaching on the pale moonlight. "Storm is moving in. They'll not risk their precious cargo for a mere storm."

"Not even in the Channel? It's not as if they'll be moving in the open ocean."

Nathan shrugged. "The Channel can be equally as dangerous as open sea."

Nora nodded. "I've never been on a ship, so I must take your word for it, Mr. Black."

Nathan waited a moment more and then carefully gripped Nora's elbow before slipping into the stream of people moving along the thoroughfare.

The smell grew worse once they were inside the throng of seamen, and Nathan felt his throat constrict. They reached the dock in question and turned off, slipping out of the crowd of people just as easily as they had slipped in. They made their way carefully along the dock, dodging crates and coils of rope and the odd drunken sailor, perched precariously against both. The wind grew sharper as they moved farther along the dock, and Nathan kept his grip firm on Nora's elbow. They had nearly reached the end of the pier, when the last ship on the dock came into view, looming out of the darkness like a sudden beacon. Nathan slowly stopped, putting his back to the stack of crates resting four feet from the ship. He looked up at the vessel, noting its worn wood and wind scarred mast poles. It wasn't a big ship, but it would do for their purposes.

Nora pressed against him, and his grip on her tightened.

"Is this it then?"

He nodded.

"And how is it that you know the captain of this ship?"

"He saved me bloody life even if he did not save me blinkin' leg."

Nathan felt Nora jump, startled, but the gravelly voice and its owner were nothing that frightened Nathan.

"Reginald Davis," Nathan said, stepping forward as the man came off the gangplank of the ship before them.

The man looked no different from the last time Nathan had seen him except for the wooden peg he stood on. He was still tall and broad shouldered with a barrel chest and beefy hands. He looked as if he should be shoveling dung from a stable rather than captaining a ship, but this was where the War Office had reassigned him after his injury. And Nathan suspected it was the perfect outfit for his fellow soldier.

"Sorry again about the leg, old chap," Nathan said then, extending a hand to his comrade. "But it's better your leg than your life."

Nora looked between them. "I believe I am not familiar with this tale."

Davis approached Nora then, bowing over her extended hand.

"Tis a pleasure to meet the honorable Mrs. Black. But allow me one question. Why the bloody 'ell did you marry this whelp when you could have had someone as charming as meself?"

Nathan saw Nora blush in the moonlight and stepped closer to remove his wife from Davis's grip.

"Because she has common sense," Nathan said, and Davis laughed.

"Shall we be aboard then, chaps?" he said, turning back to the gangplank.

It was then that Nathan noticed the ship had come alive with sailors moving along the ropes and up into the masts. It vibrated with the energy of preparing to set sail.

Davis was well ahead of them when they began their way up the plank.

"How is it that you know him?" Nora whispered.

"He was in my regiment on the Continent."

"Your regiment? But how did he get into a regiment with noblemen's sons?"

Nathan grinned. "Who said he's not a nobleman's son?"

Nora looked straight ahead at Davis, her jaw hanging slack.

Nathan called up the gangplank.

"What is it you have in mind for our rescue mission, Captain?"

Davis turned at the top of the plank, the moonlight hitting him full in the back and silhouetting his impressive person in an ethereal light.

"How do ye feel about pirates, Nathan?"

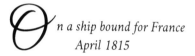

n a ship bound for France
April 1815

THE HARSH SOUND of the lock of the door grating against its metal sheath as it was withdrawn ripped apart the peace of the tiny berth that was their prison.

Alec went from blissfully lost in his wife's sleepy embrace to alert and ready. He rolled Sarah across him, jackknifing off the bed in one fluid movement. Sarah moved behind him as he stood up to get between her and whatever was coming in the door. Harpoon Man stuck his head inside.

"Captain wishes you to see," the man said in stilted English.

Alec nodded as he felt Sarah's small hand press into his back. He reached behind him and took her hand in his.

Harpoon Man shook his head.

"No woman. Just you."

Alec shook his head, too. "I'm not going anywhere without my wife."

Sarah pressed against his back now, and he gripped her hand tighter in reassurance.

"Une moment, si vous plait," Harpoon Man said and shut the door.

Alec turned, and Sarah came into his arms, resting her head on his chest.

"What do you think he wants?" Sarah whispered, her voice even softer than it had been before Harpoon Man had been so ungracious as to interrupt them.

"I don't know," Alec whispered just as softly, rubbing his cheek against her hair. His fingers found the buttons he had undone what felt like hours ago and quickly refastened them. He was not going to let those French bastards see an inch of his wife's glorious, pale skin.

They were silent then, just standing there, holding onto each other. The ship rocked gently, and the sound of water sloshing against the sides mingled with the sound of the lantern swinging on its peg. Sarah was tense against him, but he thought it was more because of the situation than any of the many problems between them, problems they had only begun to solve. He kept his arms solidly around her, not moving his hands in any attempt to soothe her. He needed soothing right now and holding onto Sarah was soothing.

"Alec?"

Alec closed his eyes, not wanting to fight with his wife any longer just then, praying that the truce they had reached earlier still stood.

"Yes?"

"Why didn't you kill him? The Earl of Wheaton. Why didn't you kill him?"

It took a moment for Alec to recall what she was talking about, but when he realized she spoke of his ill-fated duel, Alec's stomach somersaulted. He didn't know if he even had the energy to continue that particular conversation let alone the desire. But she should know why he hadn't killed Wheaton.

"I didn't want to," he said.

She eased away from him, and he looked down at her inquisitive expression. She didn't say anything, but then she didn't have to. Alec felt guilty enough to elaborate.

"I thought you might not approve if I killed him, so I refrained."

"You refrained because you were concerned about what I might think on the matter?"

Her voice was gaining back some of its strength, and Alec knew the contented mood of the moment was slipping away, the truce was crumbling. So Alec just nodded, keeping his eyes steady on her face.

And then Sarah bit her lower lip.

Alec's heart stopped momentarily. Sarah had never bit her lip. Sarah had never done anything that may have indicated that she was unsure where to step, and now her rigid exterior suddenly evaporated when Alec least expected. And that left Alec without a clue as to how to respond. He had spent four years learning how to read his wife, learning what to do and not do, and now in the space of a few hours, she unraveled everything he knew. Everything he felt certain about his relationship with her. About what he meant to her.

Thankfully, Sarah responded first.

"What I think matters that much?" she said, whispering once again and avoiding his eyes.

Alec grabbed her chin, but Sarah's eyes still looked at everything but him.

"Sarah," he said, but she still wouldn't look at him.

The sound of the lock moving again severed the tenuous connection between them, and Alec spun around, putting Sarah safely behind him. This time the door came fully open, and Alec had to shuffle Sarah back so the door didn't hit them. The captain's perfectly coifed head of blond hair appeared around the doorframe.

"Is there a problem, monsieur?" he asked.

Alec felt Sarah tremble against his back.

"I'm not leaving my wife alone."

The captain nodded and moved farther into the doorway. "I understand your position, but I must insist that you join me in my quarters. Alone, monsieur."

"Why?" Alec asked, reaching behind him to grab Sarah's hand as she shivered again.

"There are certain delicate matters we must discuss."

"The countess can join us. I assure you, Captain, women do not have the mental capacity to handle delicate matters. She will be quiet as she should be, and we can discuss whatever needs to be discussed."

Sarah poked him in the back, so he poked her in the stomach. Her soft Ow almost had him grinning.

"I still must insist, monsieur. These are state affairs that I can only discuss with you."

Alec saw Harpoon Man shift against the far wall of the passage as Sarah grabbed a handful of his coat, latching herself to him.

"Then I'm afraid we are at an impasse, Captain. I will not leave my wife."

"Perhaps you can be persuaded," Teyssier said, turning and disappearing down the passage.

Alec waited, unsure of what the captain was going to do. One of Sarah's arms came around him as the other hooked around his shoulder. He felt her drag her body up, so she could see over his shoulder.

"Where did he go?" she whispered, which actually sounded very loud as her mouth was so close to his ear.

"I don't know," Alec said, distracted by the warmth of her breath against his neck.

"Don't leave me, Alec."

"I won't," he said, irritated that she would even say that. He had left once. Just once. He did not have a chronic problem with remaining immobile.

Sarah didn't move but stayed attached to his back, her arms holding her up so that she was pressed as firmly as possible against him. Alec could have summoned the energy to ignore the fact that he liked his wife hanging onto him so tightly, as if seeking safety, but he didn't feel like ignoring it. Sarah had never held onto him when she needed strength. She had never had to. This was a pleasant change of circumstances that he was not going to dismiss.

Were things actually changing between them? Was he finally getting through to her?

But the captain returned before Alec could truly enjoy the moment. Teyssier marched through the door, stopping mere inches from Alec, forcing Alec to recoil from the stench that emanated from the captain. Sarah never let go of him and backed up with him. Teyssier extended his hand, a very distinct hat held between two fingers.

"I believe this will persuade you."

The captain smiled as a cold shiver ran down Alec's spine. He waited a breath, but Sarah did not react as he had expected her to, giving nothing away. It was the first time Alec had seen the captain smile since boarding the ship. Reluctantly and with great trepidation, Alec reached up and took the hat, flipping it over in his hands.

The last time he had seen that hat it had been atop Thatcher's head.

Alec's stomach dropped to his toes, and his throat closed. Sarah moved against him, but she made no noise. Alec's heart beat so loudly he was sure everyone in the room could hear it. He needed to form a reaction, form a response. But before Alec could react, Sarah shoved him out of the way, which wasn't very far as he ran into the wall. She squeezed around him though, snatching the hat out of his hand.

"Ou est l'homme?" she said, waving the hat in the captain's face.

The startled captain responded in English. "I do not know, madame. I will speak with your husband now."

The captain made his way towards the door as Sarah followed. Alec grabbed the back of her dress and dragged her back.

"I shall speak with you now, Captain," Alec said, tightening his hold on Sarah's dress when she opened her mouth to object. He pulled the fabric so tightly the protest turned into an undignified squeak.

"I thought you would," the captain said, having reached the door. "You must accompany me to my quarters. Alone."

"I'll need a moment with my wife. Alone," he added harshly.

"Bon," the captain said and gestured to Harpoon Man.

Harpoon Man stepped forward and closed the door, but the lock was not slid into place.

As soon as the door was shut, Sarah rounded on him, but Alec hauled her up and kissed her before anything came out of her mouth. She pushed against his shoulders, but he wasn't letting go. He kissed her hard, forcing her lips open to make her an active partner in this kiss. She was not going to disappear into herself now. He pressed her against the wall, battling with her skirts to grab her thighs so he could pull her legs up around his waist. She obliged him, wrapping her legs tightly around him, holding herself up while his hand worked on the fastenings of his trousers.

"Alec," she said, encompassing in his name everything she wanted to ask.

"I'm not going to leave you, Sarah," he said against her neck, "I am never going to leave."

He drove into her and covered her mouth with his to capture the moan that instantly rose to her lips upon his penetration. He filled her entirely with full, strong strokes, attempting to make her believe him by connecting with her in the most basic way possible.

He felt the growing tension in her body, felt her orgasm building. Moving one hand along the line of her hip and slipping it between her legs, he touched her. Sarah exploded around him. She buried her face against his shoulder, but he still heard her muffled scream. In that scream was her surrender. Alec felt it in the way her body responded to his, collapsing onto him and holding him up at the same time, giving up, giving in, and still holding her own. And he followed her, emptying himself, body and soul, into her.

He didn't know how long he held them there, suspended in what had just happened. He didn't know how he held them up. His entire body had turned to water he was sure, but his legs were solid beneath him. His grip on Sarah's legs weakened though, and he let her feet drop to the floor. He still held onto her, pinning her between the wall and himself to keep her upright. She kept her face hidden in his shoulder as she continued to shake, from the climax or from something else he wasn't sure.

"Sarah?" he said, hoping to draw her out, hoping she wouldn't pretend to be invisible right then, hoping that she wouldn't pretend she didn't exist, not when he had stated, in the most carnal way he knew how, how much he loved her and how he was not going to leave her.

"Come on, love," he coaxed, nudging her with a playful butt of his nose against her ear. "I need you to tell me you're all right."

It was not exactly what he needed to hear from her, but it would do for now.

Sarah's arms were around his neck, but they suddenly

melted, sliding down his chest. He thought she was going to withdraw physically from him, but instead her arms slipped around his waist, and she snuggled closer to him. Her back came away from the wall, and he was able to get his arms all the way around her.

"I'm all right," she whispered, barely loud enough for him to hear her.

Alec drew in a much needed breath and reached up to tilt her face up to his. He kissed her slowly, lingering in the softness of her lips. He pulled away before he wanted to and fastened his trousers. Sarah straightened her skirts, batting them down when the stiff material wouldn't fall back along her legs.

Alec waited until she was decent.

"All right?" he asked.

Sarah nodded.

"I'm not leaving you. I just need to see why Captain Teyssier has Thatcher's hat," he said carefully, no longer brave enough to touch her.

Sarah looked like she might break if he so much as brushed a strand of her golden hair behind her ear. So he turned around and opened the door.

The captain lounged against the opposite wall, his perfect hair contrasting sharply with his unshaven chin and dirty hands. Harpoon Man wasn't much better looking, and for the first time, Alec worried about leaving Sarah for reasons other than her fears.

He might seriously never make it back to this prison.

He might never make it back to his wife.

And if that were to happen, there was something she needed to know.

With his hand still on the doorknob, Alec turned partway, so that he could see Sarah standing dazed in the swinging lantern light. She looked small and utterly alone. His heart constricted even as he knew he was doing the right thing. He had to find out what had happened to Thatcher. Not for the War Office. Not for any strategy against Napoleon. But because Thatcher was his friend, and he was not going to let any harm come to him if he could prevent it.

So he was going to have to leave Sarah all alone in their prison.

But first he would give her something to think about, so she wouldn't think about him leaving.

"Sarah?" he asked, getting her attention even though she was already looking at him. "The first time we met? It wasn't on our wedding day."

He didn't wait for her reaction.

He closed the door between them.

ALEC EXPERIENCED an instantaneous need to be sick upon entering the captain's quarters. Teyssier obviously lied when he said his accommodations were better than the berth into which he had tossed Alec and Sarah.

The room smelled like old cheese and human filth. Clothes were tossed here and there. Plates of half eaten food festered on various flat surfaces. The bedclothes dripped lazily to the floor from the bunk. Wadded pieces of parchment and newsprint littered the floor. And a chamberpot in the corner was dangerously close to spilling its contents everywhere. If he did not feel such a need to help his friend if his friend indeed needed helping, he would have left immediately and returned to the slightly more desirable conditions of the prison he shared with his wife. At least, Sarah was there, and he very much wanted to be with her just then.

He had made love to her.

Again.

For only the second time.

He needed to get back to her.

But Teyssier entered the room close behind him, and he was forced to take a step farther into the mess before him.

"A chair, perhaps?" Teyssier said, unearthing one from a pile of dirty linens.

It was a standard wooden affair and did not outwardly appear to contain any food particles or fecal matter as it were. So Alec sat in it, keeping his back straight, not touching the back of the chair for fear his visual inspection was inaccurate.

Teyssier moved behind the table that took up the center of the room and which consisted of most of the plates of half eaten food. Alec swallowed as the captain rummaged through the plates, finding one that seemed to suit him, pulling it from the pile and settling in to begin eating the remains of whatever it was. Alec closed his eyes briefly and thought only of Sarah.

Thatcher was their only hope for getting out of this before the ship left the port for France. Once they were in the Channel, the chances of being rescued dropped significantly. He couldn't fail Sarah. She would never let him live with that failure, and worse, neither would he. He opened his eyes.

"I believe you brought me here to discuss that particular hat," Alec said, pointing to the garment in question, which now lay on the table beside the captain.

The captain spoke around the wad of food in his mouth. "There appears to have been a commotion in the port. I wish you to explain to me what it is about."

Alec shrugged. "I've been on this ship with you and your lovely companions. What would I know of a disturbance in port?"

Teyssier set down the plate of food and wiped his hands

on his trousers. "There appears to have been two people involved. The gentleman wearing this hat." Here he picked up Thatcher's hat. "And a rather, what is the word? I believe it to say remarkable lady."

Lady Cavanaugh. That could be the only other woman who would be in Dover and assisting Thatcher. But what did that mean? Thatcher should have been on his way to London to fetch the entire War Office if he needed to. Why was he still in Dover? And why was he with Lady Cavanaugh?

Teyssier watched him, and Alec gave no indication that any of this meant anything to him.

"The gentleman, he had an accent." Teyssier smiled, showing his teeth. "Not one as refined as mine, but an accent, n'cest pas?"

Alec did not agree or disagree.

"They say he is from the Colonies. I do not know what this may mean. A gentleman from the Colonies helping the British? It does not seem to fit. You care to explain?"

Alec cared to do no such thing and so did nothing.

Teyssier continued. "The gentleman, he follow your abductor, the one with the absurd gold teeth. He follow through the port and attempt to board the same ship he did. You know about this?"

Alec grew tired of all of the questions he could not possibly answer.

"I think it best to get to the rest of the story, Captain. I know nothing of which you speak, and I have nothing to add in commentary."

Teyssier shrugged. "I do not know if that is truth. You could be lying. Is this gentleman a part of your plan? Clearly, you recognize the hat. You must know something or you would still be with your cherie."

Alec made no motion at the mention of Sarah but said, "What plan?"

Teyssier picked up the hat again, running the brim between his fingers. "Allow me to tell you what it is I think," Teyssier said, and Alec wanted to roll his eyes in relief.

If the captain would just talk, he could learn what had happened with Thatcher and get back to Sarah.

"This gentleman, he wait in port to rescue you, only he is not sure where you are. So he follows the last person he saw you with and tries to get information. He needs this information in order to bring help. To bring people to save you. When he is stopped, he flees. And the plan to rescue you does not work."

The captain paused, and Alec did not so much as blink. Thatcher had fled. But did he make it out of Dover?

"But that may not be what all that happened. This gentleman from the Colonies. He may just be a ruse. A distraction. A lie? He may be keeping us from the real truth, n'cest pas?"

Alec did not speak.

"I do not like surprises, mon ami, and it will serve you well to tell me the truth of things now. We will be underway shortly, and things can only grow more uncomfortable for you."

Alec's mind flashed to Sarah alone in the berth, and he felt a cold tickle of dread move down his spine. She would be all right. He would get back to her. He would save them both, and everything would be all right in the end.

He would finally make her laugh. He knew he would.

"But some part of this does not make sense."

Alec could think of many parts of this that did not make sense, but that was not the point just then. The point was to end this conversation and leave. Thatcher could be all right. He had fled. He must have gotten out. Did that mean he could still formulate a plan to save them? He could not be sure, but he knew the man was alive. That was enough to allow him to return to Sarah.

"The woman this gentleman was with. She say something peculiar."

Lady Cavanaugh had said a number of peculiar things on more than one occasion. Alec did not see how this was relevant.

"She say she a countess. A countess from Italy. You know this woman."

The last part was not a question, and it was all Alec could do to keep from smiling. Yes, he did know the Katharine Cavanaugh who would pretend to be an Italian countess. But Teyssier did not need to know this. So Alec continued to say nothing.

"I see you are not going to help a friend right now, mon ami. This saddens me."

Teyssier stood, and that cold tickle of fear burning down Alec's spine erupted into flames that threatened to engulf him.

"I think it best to give you time to think about matters."

Teyssier moved from behind the table, his feet shuffling in the debris on the floor. "You must think about what is best not only for you but for your lady wife."

The captain stood close enough now that Alec could see where his beard disappeared into the stained fabric of his collar. He could smell the man's stale breath and dried sweat. He could smell entirely too much.

"You will stay here, I think, to think of these things. And then perhaps, you will wish to cooperate."

Before Alec could form a protest, Teyssier moved to the door. Alec stood, moving the chair as if to make a run for the door, but Harpoon Man stood there. Or if not Harpoon Man, his evil twin. And Alec carefully sat back down.

"You will think," Teyssier said and shut the door, giving Alec no chance to get back to his wife.

He sat down on the wooden chair. Defeat weighed on him like a fog on a hillside. There but not solid enough to grasp in one's hand to move away. He had told Sarah he would not leave her. He had told her that. And now he was stuck in the captain's quarters. He thought about trying the door handle but knew it was unlikely they would leave the bolt off.

The ship rolled beneath him, but he did not move. He sat in the chair, his mind blank except for the look on Sarah's face when he had closed the door.

He wondered if she had figured it out by then. If she knew when it was that they had first met. It was not something he had ever forgotten. And that moment in the church four years ago, when he had seen her standing there in her gown, he hadn't known what to do. The immense amount of alcohol in his system had not helped matters either. And even now Alec couldn't remember everything of that day.

But he could not forget Sarah.

There were moments in their life together that had frozen in his mind. The image of a young Sarah the first time they had met. Moonlight cascading across her shoulders as if she were a majestic sprite. Sarah at the altar, a grown woman wreathed in flowers. And then Sarah from moments before, her tattered gown clinging to her with its last threads, her hair mussed and matted, grime streaking down her face. But none of that had made the image freeze in his mind. It was the look in her eyes.

It was the look of a woman who had been thoroughly loved.

Is loved.

He suspected that last bit was his own selfishly hopeful expectations. There was a large distance between physical love, and the love he had been trying to show Sarah for so many years. And while he had definitely made love to Sarah, he doubted she felt the truth of it. He doubted she knew the depth of his emotions. She had always called him ridiculous and immature, but he had never felt that way about her.

What he felt for her was something unlike he had ever experienced. His love for his family ran deep. His father and Jane and Nathan. And likely soon to extend to an indomitable housekeeper and her son. And while his love for his family was strong, insurmountable and unconditional, it did not compare to the burst of passion that overwhelmed him whenever he saw his wife.

His love for Sarah was organic, a living, breathing thing that was always just out of his reach. It was something he moved forward for, moved toward every day, hoping that one day he would catch it. One day he would catch her.

But he never did.

For four long years.

His chest hurt. He rubbed at it as if to dispel the ache that defeat ground into him. He dropped his hand into his lap and looked at it. Red and raw from exposure, his fingers clenched and unclenched.

And then as he had done mere days before, Alec folded his hands and prayed, because he didn't know what else to do.

CHAPTER 8

*L*ondon, England
Just before their abduction

ALEC PRAYED.

He hadn't really done much praying lately, but he figured that if any situation called for divine assistance, this was it. He had done everything he could think of, everything his pathetic, unimaginative brain could come up with to make his wife laugh, to make her love him. But nothing had worked. He sat in a cold, empty church, soaking wet from having walked around London for hours in the rain, and he prayed to a god he hadn't spoken to in years.

Desperate was the word that came to mind.

Desperate to make her look at him with something other than disdain. Desperate to make her see him for a human being and not the immature whelp he knew she saw. Desperate to stop being on the wrong side of all the doors she closed in his face.

Just desperate.

And last night...

God, last night.

He raised his eyes to the ceiling momentarily and wondered if he should clarify to God that he wasn't speaking to him directly at that moment.

But what had happened?

Well, he knew what had happened, but what had driven them to it? What had driven him to it?

In four years, he hadn't so much as spoken intimately to his wife. Hell, he hadn't even spoken friendly to his wife. There had been a time when he had jested with her, smiled with her and laughed with her. But he had always fooled himself. He did none of those things with her. He had just done them in the attempt to make her realize he was there. Intimacy was this mysterious thing that happened to other people, not him. But last night, he had clearly encountered intimacy and surged right through it to carnal knowledge.

But what was he supposed to do when the woman whom he had loved since the first sight of her had suddenly, unexpectedly kissed him?

In fact, kissed did not accurately describe what she had done. She had all but devoured him. She had bit him. And stupid idiot that he was he had said Ow and nearly shoved her off the sofa. Ow was really not the best response in that situation, but she had bit him. It wasn't until she was almost to the door of the library in their townhouse that he thought to get up and go after her. And then he had happily returned the endearing show of emotion by biting her back. He knew he had probably hurt her, but the tracks her fingernails had made still burned down the length of his back.

He had reached the top of the stairs before he realized he was taking her to a bed. It was more like hauling her to a bed because she was tossed over his shoulder, but regardless of his method, his destination was clear. He was going to get his wife in a bed, and he was damn sure going to be present.

What he had not expected was to stop when he did, but he couldn't help it. He had watched her as he had stroked her to climax, and the look on her face when she broke had his chest tightening to uncomfortable proportions. Her eyes had fluttered closed, and he had felt like she had put all of her trust in him. Trusting him with her body, her heart, her very soul. And still shivering from the pleasure he had given her, she had opened her eyes and smiled.

That was when he realized he couldn't do it.

He couldn't make love to his wife as long as he knew she didn't care about him.

Her smile had been one of satiation, of contentment, of pure physical happiness.

She had never smiled like that at him before. She had never smiled at him before. And that knowledge had driven him off the bed and out the door. This time it was him who closed the door between them, but it hadn't made him feel any better standing in the hallway looking at it.

So now he sat in Greyfriars, soaking wet and probably catching the fever that would kill him, but he had suddenly felt the need to return to the scene of the crime, as it were. He stared at the altar where he had been forever tied to Sarah Beckham. He hadn't realized then that being tied to her did not mean that he would be happily tied to her. It may have been his state of intoxication at the time that kept him from realizing it, but he thought it more likely came from the secret moment he had been cherishing, nurturing for years.

The moment when he had first met the incredible woman he now found himself married to. The moment when he had stumbled upon her at the Duke of Kent's country party and fallen for her untrusting blue eyes and cynical overbite.

That was what he was thinking about when he had wed

her that day four years ago. He had been thinking Fate had finally dealt him a good hand. He was marrying the young woman whose spell he had fallen under, the young woman who had stayed unresistingly resilient, unbending, and proud in his memory. The young woman who had first made him not hate his social obligations so much. The young woman who had first shared his disdain for titles borne by people who did not deserve them.

The young woman who had caused the first stirrings of longing for a family.

Unable to look anymore, Alec stood and walked out of the church, the squishing of his wet boots drowning out the quiet sobs of the young woman hiding in the darkness at the back of the church.

* * *

London, England
Just before their abduction

SARAH STOOD inside the doorway of Greyfriars, worrying the fingertips of her gloves. The day was overcast, so candles had been lit in the torches as little light trickled through the windows. She took a cautious step forward, not picking her foot up from the floor, just sliding it across the ground and listening to the scrape of her shoe, letting the harsh sound grate her ears.

She could see Alec, sitting four pews from the front. His shoulders were hunched, and his hair was wet. She could see it glisten in the soft light. It had been raining earlier, hours earlier. She wondered how long he had been sitting there. Since he had left her? Since he had run in the middle of making love to her?

She took another step forward, the grating softer as her foot left the ground a little more. Alec must not have heard her because he didn't move. She pulled at the sleeve of her morning dress where it rubbed against her gloved palm. Feeling the lace through her gloves reminded her that she had not changed into something more appropriate.

She had left Stryden House that morning as soon as she'd discovered Alec was missing. She had gone to his father's house looking for Nora. Sarah had only met Nora the day before, but she had met the woman in a crisis, a particularly bad crisis for a mother. Nora's son had been kidnapped, but Nora was still infallible. And Sarah was convinced Nora could do anything.

But Sarah had collapsed into her agony before Nora could do anything. Awaking some time later on a sofa in the Duke of Lofton's library, Sarah still suffered from a missing husband. The Duke had promised to find his errant son, but when the hours passed without the Duke returning to his townhouse with the good news Sarah wanted to hear, or better, with Alec, she had left the house, her feet moving in a direction all their own. She hadn't realized she was going to Greyfriars until she was bathed in the light of the candles that lit its interior.

Now, she couldn't get her feet to move even with all of her energy concentrating on them, asking them to move, begging them to move toward the bent head of her husband. They just wouldn't go. As soon as her eyes adjusted to the dimness upon entering the church and had made out the unmistakable shape of Alec, her body had ceased to obey her command. It remained frozen where it was, and the most she had been able to do was shuffle a few pathetic steps. The darkness that was not reached by the candles that enveloped her, and it was as if her body was reluctant to leave its safety.

But Alec looked sad.

She wanted to go to him, sit on the pew next to him, and if her courage allowed her, take him into her arms so he wouldn't look that way anymore. She couldn't bear to see him so unhappy. Alec, happy, arrogant, unflappable, should not look as if the things he held dear in the world had suddenly evaporated out of existence, and there was no hope that they would be returned to him.

She couldn't handle the emotions that welled up in her. She couldn't handle him looking so horrible and knowing, deep inside of her, that she had made him look that way. She was sure any earl would look that way being married to a bastard like her.

But what about last night?

What had that meant?

The Earl of Stryden had carried her over his shoulder to her bedchamber, thrown her on the bed, and attacked her. But he had uttered a single word before ravishing her. And that one word had sent hope blossoming through her.

Beautiful.

He had been so serious when he had said it. So sure that what he was saying was true and sacred. She had been fascinated by his face as he first touched her. His eyes had been clear and focused, his hands steady and sure, certain of their task, certain of their duty. And as those hands had passed over her, she had become aware of that duty as well.

Cherish. Pleasure. Passion.

Love.

But he had left.

And completely left. Not just left the room kind of left but went off of the bloody map kind of left. Someone did not abandon one's post in the middle of a crisis like they had been facing. Nora's son kidnapped, nonsensical instructions to go to Dover, her husband making love to her.

These were all crisis level events, and he had wandered

off. Worse yet, Sarah could not make herself go to him. She could not bring herself to even ask him what was wrong. Any normal human relationship would have allowed for such a question, but theirs was clearly not a normal human relationship. They had been wed by direct order of the government of their country and forced to carry on a charade that suited neither of them. Not that Alec had ever said such, but Sarah knew he couldn't possibly enjoy this farce. So that left her unable to ask a simple question of the man she loved. She could not ask him what was on his mind.

Alec stood before she could start admonishing herself for her illegitimate birth and began walking toward her. She backed up farther into the shadows and held her breath.

But the tears she could not stop. The tears came anyway, coursing down her cheeks, and the worst part of it all was she was crying for something that had not yet happened. She was crying for the day she was no longer the Countess of Stryden. For the day when they would receive an official annulment. Most likely something along the lines of her inability to produce an heir. Everyone would think it so tragic, so unfair. But Sarah would know why it really was unfair, and so she cried.

Standing there in the dark, letting her husband slip past her without speaking a single syllable, Sarah allowed herself to take pity on her herself. To bemoan her situation and her existence. To hate the place where she had been put. By the War Office, by her adoptive mother, and by God himself. Sarah hated it all and hated herself even more for thinking it was just happening to her. That she couldn't stop it, that she had no power.

Sarah had never taken anything in her life. At the orphanage, she had made sure there was enough porridge in her bowl every morning. At the place she had once called home in Dorchester, she had made sure her adoptive mother never got too close to her, physically or emotionally. And she most certainly took no slack from anyone at the War Office. It was her duty to protect her country, and she would be damned if anyone fouled up the one thing she was good at.

So why then had Alec just walked out the door without her saying anything? Why had she let the one person she had been searching for leave without a care? Why was Sarah suddenly letting everything happen to her?

What the bloody hell was wrong with her?

She wasn't sure when the tears had stopped, but her face was dry when she reached the street.

* * *

LONDON, *England*
Just before their abduction

"YOU BLOODY CAD!"

Alec ducked before Sarah's flying fist could connect with any part of his person. He looked about him, at the lush grass of Hyde Park and the burbling waters of the Serpentine, and wondered for a moment if his wife was having an attack of the hysteria. He had heard that other women sometimes succumbed to its pull, but he had not expected it of Sarah. He backed up a pace and looked at her wrinkled and mussed pink gown, her hair loose in its pins, and her face streaked with—

Had Sarah been crying?

He took a step forward.

"Lady wife, to what do I owe—"

"Do not use that kind of language with me, you terribly excuse for a man."

Alec had been called many things in his life, but nothing really sunk in like a blow to his manhood.

"I beg your pardon, Sarah, I did not realize—"

"Yes, you didn't realize," she cut him off again, "You never realize, Alec. You never realize that your words and actions cause consequences, and there are people who must live with those consequences, and you cannot go about flitting through the world as if you have no impact on anyone."

Alec thought that a ripe accusation as he suspected the person he had the least impact on had spoken the accusation.

"I apologize, Sarah. I will try to do better in future. Now, what are you doing here?"

He looked about them again. He had left Greyfriars a short while before, crossed the river, strolled past St. James, and then found himself in the park, looking at the Serpentine. He wasn't even aware that he was being followed if Sarah in fact had been following him, which seemed ludicrous. Why Sarah had any interest in him he could not fathom. But she did in fact stand in Hyde Park yelling obscenities at him, so perhaps, Sarah was not as he had presumed.

"I should be asking you that question, Lord Stryden," she nearly spit at him, "What gives you the right to abandon your wife in the middle of—"

Now she stopped, and he really had been looking forward to her finishing that sentence. But Sarah looked about them instead as if briefly remembering where they stood and not wishing to tarnish her reputation to too great a degree.

"You left," she said instead of what he had hoped she would say, but he still understood her meaning.

"Yes, I did leave. I apologize for that, but circumstances as they were, I could not possibly stay."

He hoped to say nothing on the topic really as he knew he could not speak the truth without Sarah being angry with him. And he did not have the strength in him that day to have his wife be angry with him. Although, she clearly already was. But something passed across Sarah's face then, something dark and foreboding, and Alec took a step forward, his hand outreached as if whatever it had been was tangible, and he could simply lift his fingers and pull it away.

"Sarah—"

"You bastard," she whispered, the strength in her voice vanished.

Alec dropped his hand. "Nathan's the bastard, mate," he said and regretted it the moment it slipped from his lips.

"That is all that you are capable of, isn't it?" Sarah asked, her eyes flashing an icy blue.

Alec retreated a step, shifting uncomfortably from foot to foot as elegant strollers moved down the path mere feet from where they had this most indelicate conversation. He watched the strollers, imagining the whispered conversations under their parasols and behind gloved hands. He saw a duchess or two pass by as well as a marquess with her matronly dowager mother. Talk of this little chat was going to spread quickly. Not that Alec truly cared, but he knew at some point, Sarah was going to blame him for something that came out of it.

"You are only truly capable of immature and superficial relationships with the ignorant and uninteresting debutantes of high society."

This last remark was rather loud and emphasized in such an unpleasant way that Alec noticed the heads of a few strollers turning in their direction, and he knew that at least two of them were the ignorant and uninteresting debutantes to which Sarah referred.

No, perhaps it was three.

"And I cannot understand how someone as intelligent, educated and refined as yourself can bear to carry himself in such a manner. Does your lineage mean nothing to you? Does your upbringing mean nothing to you? What does your father think of your behavior?"

Something old and deep sparked inside Alec at the mention of his father. It had taken Alec everything he had as a young boy to make his father love him, to make his father forgive him for the worst of sins, for killing his mother in childbirth. The man he was today allowed him to hold onto that love. He made his father laugh, and if Alec made him laugh, he knew his father would forgive him. Even if Alec could not forgive himself. And to have Sarah question that brought up his defenses.

So he turned away from her.

He heard the sharp intake of breath from Sarah, but he continued to walk away from her down the edge of the Serpentine.

"Alec!"

Sarah shouted now, but he did not turn until she grabbed his arm and spun him around. He had not been expecting her to follow so quickly, and the sudden pull on his arm almost had him falling into the water. He grabbed at her shoulders to steady himself, but for the briefest of moments, he thought of pulling her into the water with him, and the image gave him a perverse pulse of pleasure.

"Sarah, I choose not to have this conversation with you at this place and time."

Sarah's grip on his arm tightened. "And what place and time would be convenient for you, my lord?"

He felt her hands move to his waistcoat, felt her pull at the fabric, and he looked down, unsure of what she was doing. She was already having a private conversation at higher than normal decibels along a fashionable strolling path in the middle of Hyde Park in the center of the city of

London, and he knew he could no longer guess where her polite boundaries would begin to reign in her temper.

He felt something dislodge from his waistcoat, and the glint of watery sun shone off of his pocket watch.

"Time, my lord? You prefer to do this at another time?"

Alec watched his pocket watch flash in her hands as she held it scant inches from his face.

"This is what I think of your time, my lord."

And with that she tossed the watch into the Serpentine. Alec watched the gold flash through the air before landing with a tiny plunk into the water. Annoyance boiled inside him. The watch was not an heirloom or anything, but it was still his bloody watch. And she had no right to take it and toss it into the Serpentine.

Alec turned to her and without thinking, grabbed the parasol that hung from the crook of her elbow and tossed it into the water. It fell just beside the residual rings in the water that the pocket watch had made seconds before. The water closed over it, and it was gone.

"And that is what I think of you throwing my bloody watch into the water."

Sarah's mouth hung open, her eyes wide. She stared at the place where her parasol had just disappeared, and it was a full breath before she turned back to him, her eyes angry slits.

"Wanker!"

"Shrew!" he yelled back, his hands moving to his hips.

His blood boiled now. Sarah had looked down her nose at him for long enough. If he had expected that he could ever make her love him, he had clearly been wrong. Sarah would always think she was too good for him, and no amount of frivolity and laughter would ever change that. Alec could never change that.

"I would prefer it if you could refrain from calling me

names in public, countess, but perhaps your crude upbringing prevents such politeness."

It was as if he had slapped her. The blood drained from her face, her skin going white and stark, and her breath caught in her chest. He watched it freeze as she took a step back. He had finally gotten to her. After four years of trying to get any kind of response out of her, his rash words had done it. And he hadn't even really meant them.

"Sarah?" he said, his hand once more outstretched between them as if he could remove whatever it was that had come over her.

But Sarah was already turning, moving away from him along the water, and his legs wouldn't move to follow her. He had to sprint to catch up with her, but by then she had moved a few yards down the water behind a screen of trees along the water's edge. The spot was more secluded, but it did not offer abject privacy. Still, he caught her arm and drew her around.

"You needn't worry, my lord. I shall not be calling you any names in the future."

"Sarah," he began, but she wasn't finished.

She pulled her arm away. Her voice wobbled as if she was crying, but her eyes were dry. "I apologize for any inconvenience I may have caused you, but I shall be a burden no longer. I shall go to the War Office directly and ask for reassignment. You must no longer worry on how to execute your departure from this situation."

She gestured between them as if to encompass everything that had occurred in four years.

He put his hands on her shoulders and dropped his voice as if soothing a startled animal. He did not understanding what she was talking about, but perhaps he could coax her back to him, back to sanity, at least.

"Sarah, I must beg your forgiveness. My words were careless, and I did not mean them. Please accept my apologies."

But even as he spoke she shook her head. "No, Alec. I cannot forgive you for speaking the truth. Now if you'll excuse me."

She tried to break free of his grasp and move away from him, but he did not let go.

"Sarah, please talk to me. Really talk to me. I do not know what has upset you. I do not understand. And I'm sorry I threw your parasol into the water. That was extremely childish of me."

He hoped his tone carried with it the emotion he was too frightened to put into words. But he hoped Sarah sensed it, understood it.

"Alec, you needn't worry any longer. I know it must have upset you greatly to think on how you were going to remove yourself from this arrangement, but I will take the responsibility for that endeavor. You needn't worry any longer. I know when my welcome is overrun."

Her words made absolutely no sense to him, but he was not sure how to say such to her. He knew that if he made her explain, she would get even angrier with him, and that would get them nowhere.

"Sarah—"

She wrenched free and moved back the way they had come, heading in the direction of the walking path. Her shoulders stooped, and her walk was unsure and lopsided. Alec felt the first drops of rain strike his face as he watched her dejected form move away from him.

But he could not let her leave. He could not let her leave him. The thought brought a surge of desperation to his heart. He just needed more time. Just a little more time to convince her that he was worthy of her love.

"Sarah," he called, trotting to catch up.

He made no move to grab her, though, lest he startle her into picking up her pace. And it would not do for an earl of the realm to be seen chasing his wife across Hyde Park. But Sarah stopped and turned, preventing the need to give chase.

"There is nothing more to say, Alec," she said, and her voice was flat with defeat. "Good day, Lord Stryden."

She turned and walked directly into a big bloke of a man Alec had not seen. He had been too wrapped up in his fight with Sarah to even notice the unkempt man with greasy hair. Trepidation spiked through him in a flash, and he stepped up as if to save Sarah even as the man's beefy hands came down on Sarah's shoulders.

"Ye be the earl, then?" the man said, and when he smiled, daylight glinted off of a series of gold teeth in his mouth.

Alec knew then that something was wrong, but even as he thought it, he felt the grip of another unseen man come down on his arms. He looked from side to side. It was two men, in fact, equally as unkempt and menacing.

"I believe you have the wrong chap," he said, hoping to dispel them long enough to get Sarah and flee.

They were still cut off from direct sight of the walking path, but he knew that if he could just get them into view, these men would need to back off. But Alec also knew there was something greater than these men at work here. There always was.

"Oh, I'll not be fooled, me lord. Your wifey here has been screaming your bloody title across the park. Now if you don't mind, we all is going to take a fine trip to a lovely town called Dover."

CHAPTER 9

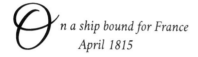

n a ship bound for France
April 1815

AFTER WHAT FELT like an entirety sitting carefully on the uncomfortable wooden chair, Alec wondered why Sarah had to throw his pocket watch into the Serpentine. It had served no purpose other than to allow her to demonstrate some anger she felt, but clearly, it demonstrated very little to him. And he very much wanted to know the time. He had gone to the bank of windows at the very back of the captain's quarters several times, but the clouds covered whatever moon there was. Shore was an indistinct blot of lights in the distance, but he knew they had not left port.

And he had not returned to his wife.

Alec leaned his head back against the hard wooden chair and felt pain spread through every muscle in his body. His shoulders ached, his arms ached, his legs ached, even the skin under his toenails ached.

But his mind wouldn't shut off, so he wouldn't have to feel the ache any more.

It was not just the physical aches of their journey, but the mental ache Sarah had aroused in him. For four years, he had tried to figure out what to say to his wife to make her love him. And every time he had tried, he had failed. And now—

He didn't know.

He had made love to her. Twice. In the span of mere days. After four years of marriage, they had finally consummated the act.

Alec lifted his head so fast he was surprised his head didn't pop off of his neck. Sarah could be pregnant. Alec felt the dread that had been simmering in his gut build to a full out boil. Sarah was alone and possibly pregnant in a prison in the dank depths of a French ship, and he had left her.

Left her.

He took a deep breath and willed his mind to calm. He didn't know what the possibility was of Sarah actually being pregnant. He just knew that it was scientifically possible that she carried his child now. An image of Sarah round with his baby sent an electric shock to his heart that had him standing up and striding toward the door.

But he stopped.

What was he going to do?

The captain had demanded his cooperation. There was no cooperation to give. He did not know why Thatcher was working with Lady Cavanaugh, and he certainly did not know why Thatcher had gone after Sven with the golden teeth.

And if he didn't cooperate, he would not be returned to Sarah.

He would be doing the very thing she had accused him of in the park right before Sven had taken them hostage. He had not thought about what she had said then until this moment.

She had been yelling a lot, and he tended not to listen when she did that. Sarah always yelled at him, and after a spell, it got rather boring.

But now he thought on it.

She was angry with him. She was angry at him for doing something.

He had figured at the time she was angry at him for violating her space. Taking advantage of her the previous night in a fit of amorous rage and then not finishing what he had started, but that wasn't right.

He had clearly taken advantage of her since then, and she had seemed to enjoy it very much. Both times.

So what was it that she had been yelling at him about?

She kept saying something about him leaving. He suddenly realized how many times those very words had left her mouth. Not always in that exact way, but nearly always with the same intent.

Sarah thought he was going to leave.

He stood in the middle of the captain's quarters on a ship in the middle of the port of Dover on his way to be sold to the highest bidder to help damn Napoleon who had returned triumphant from exile, and all he could think about was the fact that his wife thought he was going to leave.

What the bloody hell was that all about?

He was not going to do any such thing.

So why would she think that?

He sat back down, resting his head in his hands as he propped his elbows on his knees.

Sarah thought he was going to leave her. That was why she was so angry with him all the time. That was why he could not make her laugh. The crushing weight of hopelessness that he had carried for four years suddenly fell away like a drift of snow on an eave cascading down into the snowy banks below it, disappearing into a puddle of white. All of the times Sarah had told him he was going to leave suddenly made sense, and worse, he finally understood what she had been saying the park. She was going to leave before he did.

He straightened, his gaze fixated on the pile of dirty dishes on the table before him without seeing any of it.

He needed to convince Sarah that he was not going to leave her. She needed to understand that he was never going to leave her. And he couldn't bloody well do it trapped in the captain's quarters.

Alec stood and turned to the door. He pulled on the handle and found it moved in his hand. The door swung open as the ship pitched. Alec bent his knees to compensate for the tilt, letting his muscles move with the fluidity of the boat.

Harpoon Man's evil twin stood out in the passageway, this one having more hair and less teeth that Alec could plainly see as the man bared the rotted stumps at him.

"Pardonnez moi," Alec whispered, very aware of the tension in the situation, "Ou es le captianne?"

"Ici, mon ami," Teyssier appeared out of the blackness, startling Alec enough that he backed into the open door.

Alec altered his grip on the door handle as the ship moved beneath his feet.

"Sir," Alec said. "I think I should be returned to the generous quarters you have provided for me on your fine ship. I sincerely apologize that I am unable to aid you further in your confusion regarding the gentleman from the Colonies and the Italian countess. I assure you that I know nothing about that set of circumstances."

Jane had always said that you caught more flies with honey than with vinegar. He sincerely hoped that that was true now. He needed to get back to his wife.

Teyssier did not try to enter his quarters but stayed in the passageway, uncomfortably shifting against his crew member with the harpoon.

"And why is that, monsieur?"

Alec was unsure what the captain meant by that question, but he tried to formulate a response.

"I am not certain what it is you believe to be happening about you, but I can attest to the fact that there are no secret plans of rescue that I am aware of. I am completely useless to you, Captain."

Teyssier nodded, running his tongue over his lips.

Alec wanted to take a step back as his stomach rolled. There was something about a person licking his chops in Alec's general direction that upset his constitution.

"Bon," Teyssier said, bobbing his head.

"Bon?" Alec whispered, not believing that the captain would be agreeing to his request.

"Oui, I agree with your reasoning. I have no need to keep you here in my quarters if you cannot be of assistance."

Alec felt a flicker of trepidation. Something was not right.

The captain took one grimy finger and rubbed his front teeth with it. "But not right now," the captain said, looking up and moving his tongue around in his mouth.

Alec forced his teeth apart and cursed himself for hoping it was that simple, that it was that easy to be taken back to the wife he had abandoned. When this was all over, he was going to let Nathan shoot this man. He bloody well deserved it.

"Right now you will stay here." The captain smiled, his teeth just as slimy and green as before all the apparent attempts at cleaning them.

"Why?" Alec asked.

"Because I say."

The door shut in his face, and a lock tumbled into place.

Alec stared at the door and cursed himself for not listening to Sarah when she yelled at him.

* * *

AT THE AGE of thirteen years and nine months she had started riding lessons. At the age of fourteen years she had commenced Latin lessons. At the age of fourteen years and three months she had taken up watercolors. At the age of fourteen years and eight months she had broken her arm during aforementioned riding lessons.

Sarah lay on the bunk, her hands folded across her stomach, staring at the boards above her head. She gave each grain of the wood a moment in her horribly sheltered and dull upbringing after she had been adopted. She had only used up two boards.

And she still couldn't remember Alec.

At the age of fourteen years and eleven months she had stopped the Latin lessons because her tutor claimed she knew more than he did. At the age of fifteen, she commenced being extremely bored.

So she took up shooting.

The lines of grain began to blur, and she rolled onto her side. She kept her arms tightly around her stomach, unconsciously holding in the low burning pain that had begun the moment the door had closed on Alec.

Where was he? What was happening? Where was Thatcher? He was supposed to go to London. He was supposed to get help. Was anyone coming for them? Did anyone even know where they were?

She rolled to her other side, facing the doorway, watching the light of the swinging lantern cast menacing shadows about the room. She listened to the sound of the waves crashing into the wooden sides of the ship and prayed that the sea wouldn't swallow them whole. She thought a cruel jest, one God was not likely to play even on her. At least, she hoped it was not. But perhaps, God had a different sense of humor than she believed. Would he take everything away from her when she had only just begun to enjoy it?

Her husband had made love to her. Consciously made love to her. He had initiated it in fact, and she wanted to laugh at her naive, frightened self of mere days before. The one who feared waking in his arms lest she never feel it again. The sensation of security and serenity brought about by Alec's embrace gave no comparison to the look in his eyes when he made love to her. His eyes told her something no words in any language could ever begin to articulate, and the knowledge pulsed deep in her heart like a misplaced dream, faded with time but with a desire that still raged inside her.

And Alec. Her Alec.

She flinched at her own boldness, but there was something about the phrase that had to be used. At least in her mind anyways. And she would continue to use it until Lord Stryden decided to leave her.

The sound of the lock moving jarred her from her thoughts not unlike the icy fingers of the Channel had jabbed at her hours before. She rose quickly and moved to the far side of the room, putting the lantern between herself and whoever was coming through the door. It seemed ridiculous, but that lantern was her one and only defense. And if she used it, she risked setting the entire ship aflame. It was a risk she would be willing to take if it meant saving Alec. If it meant saving them.

The door slowly swung inward, its hinges protesting the weight of the heavy wooden door. A draft of stale air hit her in the face, and she sucked in a breath before she could stop herself. One of the first things Alec had taught her so many years ago was to never show a reaction no matter how great the stimulus. But Alec wasn't here now. Sarah was on her own, and she needed to practice everything he taught her if she were to see him again.

For an absurd moment, Sarah actually thought it was Alec returning, that whatever terrible plan the captain had had not come to fruition, and Alec was being safely brought back. Brought back to her. But she knew too little time had passed for that. She knew that it could not be Alec who came through the door.

And it wasn't.

It was the dark-skinned man from earlier. He shuffled under the awkward bent of his crooked back, his gnarled fingers gripping a jug between two hands. He moved to the bunk, and Sarah counted the breaths it took for him to cross the small space. It took four breaths.

"Sir?" Sarah said, unsure why the sound had come from her mouth.

She didn't have a question to ask of this man nor something to say. Why she had tried to get his attention she could not be certain. But there was something in that moment, in the movement of the swinging lantern against the crooked facade of this man that made Sarah speak.

"Sir, may I ask a question of you?"

The bent man turned to her, and Sarah thought his face likely appeared older than the man actually was. He made no sound. He simply stood, the jug held between his hands.

"Do you perhaps have the time?"

The question was utterly ridiculous in the extreme. Both for the absolute non-relevance the answer to said question would have on her current situation but also for the fact that it was unlikely a gentleman of his station would know how to tell the time let alone have a device on which to decipher it. But an uncontrollable shake had started in her fingers and had moved to her arms. She envisioned her person being

146

swamped in the unconscious tremor in mere moments, and by speaking, she had hoped to stop its progression. As unlikely and preposterous as that sounded.

But the old man did not criticize her for her question in either word or gesture. He simply turned and set down the jug next to the bunk.

"What is it you truly wish to ask, my lady?" The sound of his gravelly voice dampened the tremors in her arms. She welcomed the sound of it as it washed over her, and with it, the ethereal calm of distraction.

"I beg your pardon?" she said.

She knew what it was of which he spoke, but by evading, she could prolong this exchange. She could savor the sound of his voice, let it cocoon her in a web of diversion until Alec returned to her.

"The time is of no importance to you, and I suspect you have never requested it of anyone in your life."

It was then that Sarah noticed with what regal cadence the man spoke. She wasn't sure why this surprised her. Either because she had not noticed it earlier or because it was at all. She hoped it was the latter. The former made her sound snobbish.

"Do you know where they've taken my husband?" she asked, and again, she did not know from whence the question came.

The old man looked to his right, back at the still open door. Sarah suspected Harpoon Man lurked on the other side. She hoped this would not prevent the old man from speaking. Harpoon Man clearly did not speak fluent English. He could not possibly understand what was happening in their exchange.

The old man turned back to her, his eyes suddenly cloudy. "Your husband is in the captain's quarters, my lady. He is unharmed."

The breath left Sarah in a single, seamless exhale so robust, she waited for her body to collapse with its absence. But when her knees did not give way, she said, "Has he asked of me?"

The old man shuffled the barest of movements in her direction. "Your husband has not left the captain's quarters to ask such a question, my lady."

Sarah nodded quickly, chiding herself for being so selfish.

"But that is still not the question for which you seek an answer."

Sarah looked at the old man again. His back was still bent, and his face was still creased, but there was something in his eyes now. A light of accusation without insult, a promise of understanding without criticism.

"I don't know what he meant," she whispered, as if the old man would understand of what she spoke.

She didn't even understand it.

"I do not know yourself or your husband, but I do know this. You are both extremely skilled at speaking many words to each other, but your art of listening leaves much to be desired."

Sarah blinked.

To say she had not expected that answer was to marginalize a rather complex statement.

"I beg your pardon?" she said again.

The old man nodded even as he moved to the door. "You should listen, my lady, instead of talking. Perhaps you will hear the answer that you seek."

The old man disappeared through the door before Sarah had a chance to tell him that there was nothing there that required listening. But the door snapped shut, and the lock slid home, leaving the whine of the lantern as it swung on its hook her only companion.

She sat down on the bunk, her foot bumping the jug the

old man had left. She kicked at it haphazardly, but its hefty size kept it from moving. She looked at it as if it could provide her with answers to everything. Answers to every last thing she questioned in her life, in her marriage, in the world. As if a jug could give her answers.

Perhaps it had wine in it. If she helped herself to a healthy portion, the influence of alcohol would be enough to loosen the hold her mind had on her memories, controlling and corralling them lest they hurt her. She lay back on the bunk, letting her mind drift even as her eyes closed. The tremor moved through her arms and into her shoulders. She welcomed the vibrating sensation, welcomed the discomfort that came with it.

And she listened.

The sound of the water crashing reached her ears first, followed quickly by the whine of the lantern. She listened harder, willing her ears to reach out and pluck the sounds from around her as if they were tangible objects ready for her picking. She heard a thud in the distance, like boots hitting the floor and then treading up wooden stairs. The sound of water came again, and then the lantern swinging. She listened more. Somewhere in the ship a person sang. The slurring of words grew louder before they drifted away from her, even beyond the reach of her ears. And then there was nothing but water and the squeak of the lantern.

She wanted Alec here. She wanted to see his face, feel his touch. She wanted to goad him into saying something immature and ridiculous like he always did. She wanted him there to make her laugh.

Her eyes flew open as she sat up on the bunk, her head barely missing the ceiling above her. Realization spread through her like the warming effects of good brandy. And with it came long seething anger.

"Alec Black, you son of a—"

* * *

THE DUKE of Kent's Country Party
   July 1800

SARAH BECKHAM SCRATCHED at the lace of her collar. She didn't know why the frilly thing was considered so posh or why her guardian felt it was necessary to subject her to such torture. There was nothing wrong with a simple cotton pinafore. Her guardian said girls of her class did not wear such garments. That only those still in the orphanage would wear such a uniform. Besides, she was too old for such things. Sarah was becoming a lady, and she had to dress as such.

Sarah felt no such thing. Barely half fifteen, she still felt exactly the same as she did when she was but an eight-year-old child at St. Mary's in The City. She may have grown a bit taller and gained a bit of weight, but there was nothing about her that said she was a lady. And why was her guardian always going on about class? Sarah had no time for such things. She knew who she was, and she needn't be reminded every time her guardian told her she belonged to a different one now. Bastards never changed classes, and her guardian should've known that. Funny how no one told her.

Sarah had tried to tell her a time or two, but her guardian had simply muttered some words Sarah didn't understand but presumed they indicated her fresh behavior. She didn't see what was fresh about pointing out someone's mistake. It seemed like simple courtesy to her. But what did she know? She spent her first eight years pulling scraps of food from garbage piles and dodging carriages in the muddy streets. You could stick her in all kinds of lace, and she was still just Sarah, parentage unknown.

And if her guardian had stopped having such inflated notions about what Sarah would one day be, she would not now find herself in such a position that required sneaking through ducal gardens in the middle of the night to find said duke's famed library. If her guardian had just left her at home while she herself attended his country party, Sarah would never have been tempted by such rumors that included tales of stacks that ran four stories high. Sarah knew this rumor to in fact be a lie. The Duke of Kent's country home was only three stories high, and therefore, the stacks could only progress for the height of the manor house.

Unless there was a secret floor beneath the ground. Sarah had not accounted for that.

She hurried more quickly along the path that she felt was headed in the correct direction. It circled around from the east wing, which contained the nursery in which Sarah had been imprisoned, or offered quarters in, depending on whom one asked, and snaked its way through some decadent shrubbery, veering in the general direction of the main house. If her calculations were accurate, she would be approaching the rose gardens that were situated off of the library in question.

The moon was full and lit her path with more brilliance than she could have hoped for. The night was silent except for the odd call of an owl and the sound of the wind moving through the shrubs. She had thought she heard the sound of running feet a time or two and the strange sound of a faded giggle, quite feminine in nature, but she dismissed the noises as her imagination rearing up on her. She did not have time for her imagination to do anything and had plodded on. She rounded the last row of hedges and came to a stop, taking in her surroundings.

Several paths converged at that point just as she had expected. She rolled her right shoulder back, the stiffness from her horse riding injury settling into her bones. She tweaked it without really noticing as she decided which path to take from there. That was when they found her.

There were three of them. All tall and gangly, not quite men but no longer boys either. Their clothes were rumpled, collars loosened and buttons half done. They all had dark hair and were rather plain, Sarah noted, before she turned to move down the path from which she had come. But she was not quick enough. They had already seen her.

"What do we have here, gentlemen?" one of them said.

His voice was deeper than Sarah had expected, more man than boy, and she felt the first trickle of fear drip down her spine. Sarah was no child. She knew what men did to helpless women. Women who went places unchaperoned.

"That's the Beckham chit. My mother told me of her. Lady Barnstead adopted her or some such nonsense. Says she's leaving this girl her fortune."

"Fortune?"

This was from another one. This one was a touch taller than the rest, and his position slightly in front of the others led Sarah to understand he was the leader of the pack.

"I don't care what fortune she has or will have. She's still a trollop, isn't she? That's what her mother was. Isn't that right, gentlemen?"

The trickle of fear that had been working its way down her spine vanished in almost an instant. Rage simmered inside her. The boy may have spoken the truth, but it was a truth that did not settle well on Sarah's shoulders. It made her twitch with an unfulfilled desire to land her fist in someone's face. But there were three of them and only one of her, so she took a step back.

"Where are you going, my lady?"

Her anger twitched. The last part had been spoken with a sarcasm so plain, she expected it to get up and walk about as if it were human. She clenched her teeth and dug her nails into the palms of her hands.

"Gentlemen," she said with equal sarcasm, "I was on my way to the library. You know. A room that houses books. I'm sure you've never heard of it."

While the remark was well placed, it did not fulfill her desire to hit something, and her anger boiled on.

The leader of the pack stepped toward her. Sarah would not back up. Her pride would not allow her. The boy came closer and closer still. Sarah's heart raced, and her mind flashed to the pain a blow could cause. So many times had her cheek been struck by the sisters in the orphanage. She girded herself for another such slap, but one never came.

Instead, a fourth boy did. Right out of the hedge in a somersaulting catastrophe of limbs, dust and foliage. Sarah stepped back to avoid being trampled and waved her arms in front of her face to dispel the sudden cloud of dust. The three boys who had stopped her on the path backed up as well, coughing from the dirt the fourth boy's spectacular entrance had kicked up.

The boy stood, and the moonlight hit him like a spotlight from the sky. Sarah knew the breath had frozen in her chest, but she would deny it if anyone called her on it. The boy was magnificent. She didn't know what it was that tugged at her stomach or made her feel suddenly wobbly, but there was something about this fourth boy that called to her. And it was more than his carefully put together visage. It was his presence. Or lack thereof as it were.

"Oh, hello, mates!" he said over brightly. "Do beg your pardon, chaps. Beg your pardon. Beg your pardon. Beg your pardon."

He said this to each of the three boys in turn as he bowed to each of them. Sarah had yet to see his face in its entirety, and she moved just a bit to see if she could take in more. Her movement must have startled him, because he spun around so quickly, he knocked into her.

Sarah instinctively tucked in her recently healed arm as she prepared to be tossed on her rump, but he caught her at the last moment, his hands firm on her shoulders.

"Oh, I do beg your pardon—"

He stopped, his eyes growing huge and round, and—

Green. They were breathtakingly green eyes. Sarah blinked, but their intensity was all the same when her eyes adjusted once more. He was...beautiful.

"My lady!" he said with a grand sweep of his arm and an expertly executed bow.

Sarah did not say a single word. She had forgotten all of them.

"I do hope you accept my apologies. You see, I was on my way—"

He stopped again and turned back toward the other three boys. "Oh, I'm sorry, chaps. I'm probably in your way, am I not? How inconsiderate of me. We will just get out of your way here."

At some point the fourth boy had taken hold of her arm and now steered her away from the other three boys in the direction of the rose gardens. Sarah allowed herself to be taken along, pulled in the wake of this mesmerizing boy. She had never felt what it was that she felt now, and she didn't know what to do. She just let herself be led.

"Have a good night then, chaps," the fourth boy said as they slipped behind the hedge separating the rose garden from the path. The boy held her arm and moved quickly, disappearing deep into the gardens before stopping abruptly and looking back over his shoulder. The whole time he never loosed his grip on her arm. And Sarah never stopped staring.

"You really shouldn't go traipsing about in the middle of

night unchaperoned. You're likely to run into hooligans like myself."

He turned his attention back to her and smiled, the moonlight striking his brilliant white teeth.

Sarah still did not speak. Or blink.

"They didn't hurt you, did they?" he asked, and the concern in his voice finally snapped her back to attention.

"How dare you," she said, wrenching her arm from his grasp.

He blinked at her but otherwise did not move. "I beg your pardon, my lady, I was trying to—"

"I am not a lady, and you will do well not to call me such."

Her voice was flat with the anger she had not been able to release on that boy who had so carelessly demeaned her person.

"Is there something else you'd like me to call you? Because if you're having trouble, I can think of a few suitable names."

Her outrage came out in a strangled gasp and finally her anger released in a right cross, her newly healed arm protesting through the entire swing. Her fist caught him squarely in the eye socket, and the moment she felt her flesh connect with his, she regretted her actions. But the boy did not howl in pain. He made hardly a noise as he gripped the side of his face and staggered away from her.

"I was only trying to make you laugh," he said as he blinked at the ground, his hands on his knees.

Sarah did not stay to ask him what he meant.

CHAPTER 10

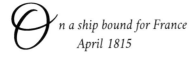 *n a ship bound for France*
April 1815

"HE WAS TRYING to make me laugh," Sarah said to no one in particular, as there was no one in the berth with her except the lantern and the jug at her feet.

She held her head in her hands, elbows perched on her knees. Her hair hung in filthy curtains by the sides of her face, and she peered through them at the lines of light created by the lantern on the floor of the berth. Her mind felt as if an infestation of ants had invaded and set up home, but there was nothing she could do about it. An entire marriage of events came rushing back to her all at once, overwhelming her in capacity and depth.

Alec was trying to make her laugh.

But what for?

She had never seemed like an unhappy person who required a spot of fun to lift her spirits. She had always thought of herself as rather polite, positive and simply nice.

Why did she need so much cheering? But there was something in the tone of Alec's voice that night in the gardens when he had told her he was just trying to make her laugh. There was more there than just a basic desire to cause fun. There was a need, a primal need, that said if Alec did not accomplish this, all was lost. Sarah didn't understand, but she was beginning to understand that the problem with her husband was not his noble birth. It was the fact that she did not understand him.

In four years, she had never listened to him. She had always assumed the meaning behind his words instead of listening to the meaning of his words. It had only taken a kidnapping and exile on a ship in the middle of the English Channel for her to realize it.

Sarah lay back on the bunk, her feet dangling over the side as the ship swayed beneath her. She felt the water getting rougher beneath her and wondered if this was the bad weather they had been expecting. For the briefest of moments, she pictured the ship going down in the stormy waters, of never seeing Alec again. But the pain it brought was swift and unkind, and she quickly pushed the thought away.

Alec had been trying to make her laugh.

All of those times she had thought he was being immature, ridiculous and poking fun at her lowly class was not at all true. He was just trying to make her laugh. Why was he so desperate to make her laugh though? She didn't have the answer to that question, and she knew she would not get it if she did not ask her husband outright.

She let out an exhale, blowing the strands of hair that had fallen along her forehead up into the air.

But first she had to get out of this damn prison. She had to get them out of this damn prison.

But seeing as how their prison was a ship floating in the

middle of a body of water, she did not have the first clue as to how to go about it. She let the water roll beneath her and the ship to carry her up and down.

She had finally realized what her husband had been saying to her for four years, and he wasn't here so she could tell him.

And that just summed up their entire relationship right there. They never told each other things. Alec did not talk, and Sarah simply yelled at him. They never did any listening.

She turned her head in the direction of the door, wondering where the old dark-skinned man had come from and how he knew so much. She wondered, too, if she could get him off this ship when the time came. She didn't know his name, but it did not matter. She felt deep down that he was an ally, and when rescue came, because it was going to come, she needed to make sure he came, too.

But as she turned her head back to the boards above her, rescue seemed like a mirage, a glimmer of hope in the distance but nothing solid enough to grab hold of. It was just there, taunting her. Keeping Alec from her.

Sarah stood up and paced. The rocking of the ship made it difficult, but the feelings inside of her kept her from sitting still. She needed action, craved it like a person in the desert craves water. She would simply die if she did not see Alec again and see him quickly. The ship pitched, and Sarah put out a hand to catch herself. The movement had the floorboards coming precariously close to her face, and Sarah knew the storm was upon them. But as the floorboards swam closer, the light of the lantern swung off the jug the old man had placed on the floor.

Sarah watched it, unmoving in the pitching waters. It must be heavy. It must be very heavy.

She quickly made her way over to the bunk, cautiously keeping one hand on a wall at all times while her feet slid across the floor. She sat on the bunk and pulled the jug closer to her. It was heavy and solid and—

She hefted it up. She could just lift the bulk with two hands, but she was fairly certain that with enough practice, she could handle it deftly. She swung it back and forth in her hands, moved it from one palm to another. Yes, it was indeed heavy, but as she worked with it, it became less cumbersome.

With each move, her confidence grew until she stood, sliding across the room with the jug between the fingers of one hand. She came to rest upon the opposite wall, just beyond the reach of the door should it swing open. She crouched against the wall, the jug resting on a bent knee as she waited. She counted her breaths, inhaling and exhaling as Alec had taught her. He said if she just concentrated on the simplest of things the rest of the world would drop away, and that one thing would become everything. And then she could focus on it, and it would not seem impossible.

So she stayed there crouched against the wall as the ship rolled and waited according to the beats of her breath.

And then she screamed. She screamed as if there was nothing holding her back. As if the very terrors of childhood nightmares had come to life and stalked her now. She screamed as if it were the only way to see Alec again.

The lock in the door began to move almost immediately, but Sarah did not stop screaming. The pitch of the ship was in her favor, and as Harpoon Man's head came into view, the ship dipped suddenly, bringing Sarah ever slightly above the man's head. With all the strength she had left, she lifted the jug and swung.

And even she could marvel at the finesse of the arc she put into it. The jug swung perfectly, hitting Harpoon Man directly on the crown of the head. He fell to his knees, dazed but not defeated. Sarah moved quickly, holding onto the handle of the door to steady her in the rolling room. Raising the jug one more time, Harpoon Man lifted his eyes to her. She looked at him and unflinchingly, dropped the jug once more upon his head.

He fell all the way to the floor then, groaning as he held his head in his hands. Sarah backed out of the door.

"Sorry about that, mate, but you should never trust a lady."

And with that, she brought the door closed and snapped the lock into place.

She stood in the corridor, inhaling drafts of stale, rotten air. She concentrated on her breath again, the jug hanging limply from her fingers at her side. It was a handy little weapon, and as her journey was far from over, she was going to keep it in reach. Her heartbeat pounded in her ears, and for a while, it was the only noise she could hear. But again, she concentrated, allowing all else to retreat, until her ears began to pick up the slightest of sounds.

But there were no running footsteps.

She had expected someone to come running at her screams, but there was no one. The ship rolled again, and Sarah presumed they were all above deck, manning the ship as the storm passed.

She had never been in the belly of a ship such as this before, and she looked to her left and right, hoping divine realization would come to her as to where she should go. But there was nothing but blackness and the occasional scurry of rats. The rats seemed to be going down though, and she thought it likely they knew where the food stores were. So she turned the other way, back in the direction she had thought they had come, and sought out a staircase that would lead her up.

The first room she came upon was filled with hammocks. She peered into the darkness at the ghostly moving shapes, but as she scanned, she determined they were all empty.

Everyone was indeed above deck. For the barest of moments, she wondered how bad the storm really was, and if she should properly worry of it. But then she dismissed it. She needed to find Alec. That took precedent over all.

Moving quickly again, she crossed the small room to the corridor beyond and this time, found stairs leading up before her. She moved the jug to her left hand and went to grab the railing when a hand closed on her arm. The scream stuck in her throat as she turned, jug raised to strike. She caught herself at the last moment when she saw the creased visage of the old man.

"It will lead you into the lion's den," he said. "You must follow me."

And with that he turned and disappeared farther along the corridor into the darkness. She didn't know how he knew where he was going, but she followed him, the light disappearing behind them. She thought the walls were closing in on her, and she pushed back at them with all the mental energy she could summon. Faintly, she could make out the shape of the old man shuffling before her. He was a small shape in the darkness, all bent and compact. But his gait was steady, a step and then a slide as he brought his other foot to. And they kept moving.

When light began to appear in the distance, Sarah thought it a part of her imagination. But then the light grew stronger, real and sure. The old man stopped in the middle of it, looking up. Sarah came to stand next to him, the jug swinging at her side as she too looked up. There was a hatch here, and the faint light came in around the cracks like a beacon across a gloomy moor.

"Is this the only way out?" Sarah asked, looking down at her bent companion.

He nodded. "You must climb out. You are capable."

Sarah was glad he had such confidence in her, but it was

not her person she worried over. It was how she was going to get him out.

"Sir, we must find another way. I need to—"

"You must find your husband and leave this ship. And you must do so now. Go, my lady."

The light struck his face at an angle, distorting the already mottled image of the bent man in the darkness. And it was something in his words that convinced Sarah that he was right. She must go. She must find Alec.

"I will come back for you," she whispered, but the man did not say anything.

Sarah set down the jug and reached up, finding the latch on the door. She turned it and pushed up. The force of the wind that struck her knocked her back, and she had to let the door close so she could steady herself. It was a magnificent storm indeed, and she was about to throw herself into it to find the man she loved. She looked once more at the old man.

"Thank you," she said.

And he nodded.

"The captain's quarters are at the rear of the ship, my lady. I bid you God speed."

He turned and disappeared into the darkness.

Sarah lifted the latch once more, and this time she was prepared when the wind struck her.

* * *

WHEN HE HEARD CANNON FIRE, he thought he was going mad sitting in the torturous wooden chair in the captain's putrid quarters. When he heard the second boom, he knew he was. He made it to the bank of windows along the far wall in four strides, but it did him little good. The storm was upon them now, and the blanket of clouds squelched what little moon there was. He kept his feet planted and his arms braced against the walls as the ship pitched beneath him, but he heard nothing more. Thinking he was indeed going mad, he made his way back to the wooden chair, his journey more difficult as no compulsion drove him forward.

Until the third boom of cannon fire.

He wheeled around in the direction of the windows so quickly, he nearly fell into the overflowing chamberpot. He righted himself just as the door to the captain's chambers opened. He stayed where he was as two men moved into the room. Alec stiffened at the sight of them. These were not the hired mercenaries with harpoons. These men looked like trained soldiers of the French navy. Their clothing, although stained and wrinkled, was not torn and appeared rather fine. Their bearing indicated they were military men, drilled in the art of physical mechanics.

And they carried guns instead of harpoons.

Big ones.

Something was wrong.

The first thing his mind stopped on was Sarah. She was alone in the berth below decks, and he needed to get to her. He eyed the men before him and knew that if he did not come up with a plan quickly, he would be out of time. Sarah could get hurt. Sarah could get killed even. His mind raced past that thought as quickly as it had come to it, as if even the very mental image of it scared him beyond sensibility.

"Hello, mates," he said, smiling as much as he could force himself to.

The taller of the two men stepped forward, motioning with his musket. "The captain wishes you on deck. March," he said.

For a second, Alec felt as if he were once more on the field under his old commanding officer, Hurst. No one had told him to march in a very long time.

"I beg your pardon, mates, but it seems I will need a little more information before I can do anything. Especially march," he said, and although his tone was light, he kept his expression firm.

The taller one looked behind him to his comrade who was making a study of his shoes instead of staying alert to the situation. Alec shifted his weight, preparing himself for whatever might come next. If the soldiers hesitated even a moment, he would take advantage of it and make his move. He had to get to Sarah. He had to get to his wife.

The taller man said something in stumbled French, whispered so gutturally that even Alec couldn't make it out. He shifted again, moving himself an entire step closer to the door without seeming to have moved at all. The shorter man said something in exchange, and finally, the tall man turned back to Alec. The ship still pitched beneath them, and he took this into consideration. If he needed to, he had the element of surprise and the constant, unpredictable tilt of the ship.

"There is a small problem. We need you on deck. The captain say so. You come with us now," he said.

Alec shook his head slightly. "Not without my wife."

The taller man gestured to the door with his gun again. "They get her now, too. You come."

Alec paused and took that in. They were bringing Sarah up from the prison below. If he could get them out in the open, he thought they might have a chance at escape. Unless the cannon fire he had heard was real, and then perhaps, there were other possibilities to consider. Such as the one in which Thatcher had made it to his father in time, and the entire British navy was there to rescue them. That somehow did not sit right with him, but he still held on hope. He had no other choice. He could not picture a world without Sarah, not when the last thing she would remember of him was how he had left her.

The tall man gestured again, only this time the point of his musket came too close to Alec for his comfort. He quickly held up a hand.

"I'm marching, mate," he said and moved carefully in the direction of the door even as the ship moved beneath them. He kept his stance wide as he made his way into the corridor. He felt the first stirrings of a breeze as he passed into the wheelhouse but was careful to hide his reactions from the sailors they met there. These chaps were more hired types, and he couldn't be sure what their reactions would be if he tried anything. He kept his feet moving forward until he reached the quarterdeck.

The wind hit him as hard and accurate as Sarah's right cross. The rain came down sideways and struck him in the forehead, cheeks and chin. He grabbed at the lapels of his jacket, as if holding the tattered garment to his person, he may find some protection from the fierce weather.

"Bloody Christ," he muttered, even though there was no one to hear. The wind carried his voice immediately up and away, and the sound was lost to the world.

He tilted his head down and pressed forward. He saw the captain's faint, squat outline a few feet ahead of him, a dark silhouette against the shadow of the wheel behind him. The captain shouted to a man beside him, another soldier, and Alec wondered what had happened to all the harpoon men. They had seemed to be in abundance when they had first boarded, but for some unsettling reason, they appeared to have vanished. Alec gripped his coat tighter against him and willed his strength toward Sarah as if on some mental level she would know that he was trying to get to her, that somehow she would know that he finally understood what she meant. It was an absurd thought, but it was the only thing driving him forward. Sarah had to know that he understood, and that he was not leaving.

The captain must have seen Alec, because he abruptly stopped talking and turned to him, beckoning him with a hand. Keeping his head bent, Alec carefully approached him, trying to see through the driving rain. He counted eight soldiers on the quarterdeck, but those were just the ones he could see. He didn't know who was below or above them, and he didn't know if the mercenaries were still fighting for their employer. Or if a new employer had suddenly come into play. When Alec reached him, the captain pointed out to sea on the starboard side.

"Friends of yours, mon ami? I believe you betray me, mon ami. I am most hurt."

Alec turned his attention in the direction the captain pointed, but all he saw was pelting rain, striking his eyes even as he tried to see into the blackness. But then there it was, materializing out of nothing and looming larger than the frigate on which he stood. It was a magnificent ship, and it lingered just off the starboard side. Alec blinked into the rain as he tried to make out its colors, but he could see no more. The masts disappeared up into the sky and seemed to end in nothingness. He looked back at the captain.

"If they're friends of mine, I have yet to be informed of it," he said, pitching his voice over the sound of wind and rain.

"Three cannons they shoot over my bow. They must be friends of yours."

Alec looked back at the ship, a suspicious feeling of relief moving through his body. There had been cannon fire. Perhaps the mysterious ship did carry men he called friends.

"I beg your pardon, Captain, that I cannot be of further assistance."

The captain's eyes narrowed, and even in the dim light, Alec could see his expression harden.

"You are conveniently unhelpful when you wish, mon ami. How is this possible?"

Alec shrugged his shoulders, a casual smile coming to his lips. "Years of practice, Captain," he said.

The captain turned away, yelling orders in French. But although the orders sounded demanding, Alec did not miss how the sailors were slow to move as if they had already determined this was a fight lost. Alec looked back in the direction of the mysterious ship to the starboard side as if he could see more to learn of its nature and calling. But there was nothing visible in the darkness, and the rocking of the ship drove him back toward the wheelhouse.

He felt the wood of the ship come up against his back, and he waited, watching the movement of the sailors around him. The storm demanded most of their attention, and Alec took advantage of it to slip farther back along the quarter-deck. He stopped in the farthest corner of the quarterdeck on the starboard side without entering the bridge. He watched there, looking for any hatches in the deck from whence they may lead Sarah from below deck. He could see hardly anything at all in the dim and rain, but he kept searching. He had to get to her. He had to tell her he was never leaving.

The ship pitched heavily, and Alec looked up in time to see a barrage of grappling hooks come over the side of the ship. He ducked, backing into the corner lest a stray hook catch him in the head. It would not due to die on Sarah before she had a chance to properly scold him for leaving her in their prison.

But as soon as the grappling hooks caught hold, chaos broke out on the quarterdeck. The captain yelled useless orders as mercenaries and sailors alike fled the quarterdeck to the main deck below. Alec eased his way in the direction of the stairwell that he thought would lead to the main deck.

Perhaps if he got lower, he could find a way down to get Sarah before whoever was on the other side of those grappling hooks decided to pay a visit.

But it was just in that moment that the gods seemed to come together, laying their calming hands across the sea as the storm suddenly blew out like an exhausted candle. The wind stopped whipping, and the rain fizzled to a light mist. And in the quiet came a noise. A voice actually. A voice that brought such intense and immediate joy that Alec's breath froze in his chest.

"Hear ye, maties," it said, "We come lookin' for something that's not yours to take, and we be 'aving it back now, ye see."

Alec dared to peek over through the railing of the quarterdeck to locate the source of the voice, and when his eyes fell on his brother, dressed to the nines in what most surely was the worst pirate garb he had ever laid eyes on, Alec breathed an intense sigh of relief.

"We have nothing that is yours," Teyssier shouted, and Alec watched as Nathan smiled a right proper smile for a pirate.

"Then prepare to be boarded."

CHAPTER 11

*A*lec freely rolled his eyes at his brother's preposterous words. Did he even know if pirates actually said that? It was not as if he made a habit of conversing with pirates. He didn't even know if Nathan had ever met a pirate. However, pretending to be a pirate was most certainly something Nathan would do.

Alec scanned the deck of the other ship, but no one person caught his eye. The chaps appeared to be Englishmen, of that Alec was certain. It was in their bearing. A well-bred Englishman never lost his bearing even when playing pirate. But the other ship swelled with men, and Alec suddenly looked back at their own ship. The mercenaries and sailors had all but vanished, leaving the ship to toss helplessly in the sea. The captain had disappeared, and the wheel spun lazily unattended.

A small group of mercenaries bandied about at the edge of the wheelhouse. They were a loose group that appeared only to relish a fight and not so much a loyal bunch bent on serving their paid duty. Alec took note to stay out of their way. He had to find his wife, and it would not do to end up dead while doing so.

His scan moved up to the poop deck and onto the riggings of the mast. A man stayed in position here and there, but compared to the mass on the opposite ship, it was obvious Nathan's men would not meet with much resistance. It appeared that the mere sight of a solidified front was enough to scare off even the paid soldier. Especially when the solidified front contained pirates.

Alec looked back at the opposite ship in time to see the first of the so-called pirates gain purchase on the grappling hook lines. They made their way across the short span of water that separated them as if they were taking a leisurely stroll in the gardens of the Queen's House. With an ease unknown to Alec, the men maneuvered onto the ship despite its rocking. He stood when the first English soldier touched the quarterdeck, stepping out from his hiding place and into the path of a soldier who looked more capable than most. At least, he did not appear to still be in knee pants as so many soldiers now did.

"It's a pleasure to see you, mate," Alec said, stepping fully in front of the lad.

Alec knew his appearance was startling at best and deplorable at worst, but he still did not expect the young man to step back as he did, sword raised at the ready. Alec quickly held up both hands. "Earl of Stryden," he said, eyebrows raised in all innocence.

The sword lowered but only by a fraction. "You're to come with me then, sir," he said, already extending a hand as if to take Alec by the arm.

Alec stepped back. "I'm not leaving without my wife, and she's somewhere below deck. I must find her immediately."

The young soldier shook his head even as Alec spoke. "I've got orders. You need to come with me, my lord."

Alec took another step back. "I'll come just as soon as I find her. But in case you're lurking about these parts, she's short and blonde and rather shrewish if you get on her wrong side. She also has a mean right hook, so watch out for that."

He turned around, prepared to go down the stairs to the main deck to see if he could find his way back down to the lower levels when he ran squarely into a barrel chest so completely solid he bounced off.

And smiled.

"Reggie," Alec said, backing up to get a better look at the man who had fought beside him on the continent. "Playing at pirates, are we now?"

Reginald Davis looked every inch the pirate right down to his wooden peg leg. He fit the picture of any child's fantasy of buccaneers on the high seas, and Alec stopped to enjoy the sight.

"I wouldn't have thought you would make a good seaman," Alec said.

Reggie sneered. "I wouldn't have thought you would make a good spy," Reginald Davis said in return.

Alec would have laughed if he were not already moving in the direction of the stairs. "Life is full of unexpected things, is it not?" he said.

"Your dear brother wants you off this ship," Davis called after him as his foot hit the first stair.

"I'm not going off the ship without my wife," he shouted back and dropped more than walked down the remainder of the stairs to the main deck.

There were more English soldiers here than on the quarterdeck, and the numbers of them alone took care of what little resistance there was still left in the paid mercenaries and the weary French sailors. The noise of battle grew louder than the sound of the sea around them, and Alec welcomed its confusion. He needed to find Sarah, and he needed to find her quickly. If not for her own safety, then for his own peace of mind. It had been too long since he had seen his wife. Any number of things could have happened to her, and he had imagined just about all of them.

He rounded the bottom of the stairs to look back along the ship for any signs of a hatch when a hand descended on his shoulder.

"Get off the ship."

Alec looked at his brother the pirate.

"I need to find Sarah," he said, turning back to scan the stern of the ship on this level.

Nathan spun him around. "You get off the ship. We'll find Sarah. It's too dangerous for you to stay on board."

Alec pulled his shoulder away. "I'm not leaving without her."

Nathan pulled off his elaborate hat with the excessive peacock feather dangling from one side to scratch violently at his scalp. "Why people wear these infernal things, I cannot fathom."

He jammed the hat back on his head. "Now listen, little brother. I did not race across the blinking English country-side to play dress up like a little girl to have you get yourself killed because of your stupid pride—"

"It's not pride, Nathan," he said, cutting off his lecture. He knew when Nathan referred to him as little brother that the rest of the speech would not be decent in the least, and he did not have time for it. "I love her, and I'm not leaving her."

Nathan stilled even as the ship rocked. "You said that out loud, you know."

Alec nodded. "And I said it out loud to Sarah as well."

"No, you did not," Nathan returned instantly.

Alec raised an eyebrow. "I most certainly did. And I'll say it again just as soon as I find her to do so."

"You told your wife that you love her?" Nathan asked.

Alec felt his frustration growing. Both at being prevented from finding Sarah as well his brother being unable to believe him when he said he had told his wife that he loved her.

"Yes, I told her that I loved her."

"And?" Nathan prompted.

Alec sighed. "And I think she's beginning to believe me."

Nathan tilted his head, adjusting the way he looked at Alec. Alec raised his chin a little higher.

"Did they hit you on the head with something?"

Alec only blinked and turned away to go back to his search for Sarah.

"Hang on there. Hang on there just a minute," Nathan said even as he spun Alec back around with a hand to his shoulder.

Although they were nearly the same size, there was something about Nathan having always been the big brother that made Alec succumb to his prodding. He wished he would not do so now, but it was a hard habit to break. Especially when he was counting on that brother to save them.

"You said she's beginning to believe you," Nathan said.

Alec nodded. "Yes, I believe that to be true."

Alec looked over Nathan's shoulder at the battle being raged behind them. Although most of the mercenaries had fled to the bowels of the ship, there were still a few dozen sailors doing their best against the highly skilled English pirates. This was not the most opportune moment to have this conversation, but it appeared it would continue.

"Perhaps she didn't understand that statement."

Alec looked back at his brother. "Didn't understand the statement? What the bloody hell does that mean? What is there not to understand about I love you?"

"I love you, too, little brother," Nathan grinned at him.

Alec rolled his eyes again. "Will you please just let me go find my wife now?"

Nathan grabbed his arm again, dragging him in the direction of one of the grappling lines. Alec fought back with everything he had, fueled by an instinct so natural and strong, he doubted anything could break it. He wrenched free, shouting at Nathan. "I told you. I am not leaving this ship without my wife."

He had never yelled at Nathan before, and it stopped his brother mid-step.

"I'm sorry, Alec. I cannot let you do that," Nathan said, stepping forward, arms raised as if to get Alec in a hold to bodily carry him off the ship.

Alec raised his fists ready to fight back when Sarah suddenly stepped between them.

"Well, aren't you two just a fine example of British intelligence," she said, and Alec dropped his fists, the air rushing from his lungs.

She was all right. She was fine actually. Standing perfectly erect, no sign of injury or duress. Absolutely beautiful in the weak light of the moon.

"Would you mind continuing this wrestling match later?" she asked, "I, for one, would very much like to get off this ship."

SHE STARED at her husband

At first she did not believe what she had heard.

And then she thought it likely her husband had gone mad.

Perhaps they had tortured him incessantly in the time they had been separated, and it had done something to his mind. Perhaps he had snapped just to cope with the physical agony. That could be the only explanation.

She stood on the deck of the ship that had been their prison, in the middle of a full battle that appeared to be occurring between French sailors and pirates in the middle of the English Channel, and she just stood there, letting the wind whip at her hair and tear at the ragged remains of her dress. She stood there and stared at her husband, not knowing what to think.

"You didn't leave," she said, and despite the noise about them, she whispered the words, afraid to speak too loudly lest the moment vanish and her hopes vanish with it.

Alec stood in front of her, the wind pulling at the lapels of his soggy jacket. He was fine. He looked fine. Not hurt, not tortured, not—

Something far worse for which she had no name. He was just Alec. And he was all right, and he was not leaving.

He was not leaving her.

It was as if something weighty and solid slid into place in her head and more importantly, her heart. It was as if something that had been not quite right for so long, something repressed and denied was suddenly let free, let free to move around on its own. Free to be as it was.

And what it was, was love.

She knew that now.

Standing there on the deck of a French ship, if not in absolute peril at least close enough to it to not be simply standing there. But she could not move. She could only stand there and stare at her husband, listening to the echo of his words in her head.

I am not leaving this ship without my wife.

"Alec, I—"

"I'm not leaving you, Sarah," he said, suddenly springing forward to grab her hands in his.

His hands were icy and rough, but she did not flinch from his touch. She looked at the tangle of their hands and felt an incredible warmth spread through her, seeping slowly and certainly into her core.

"I should have listened to you. In the park. When you threw my watch in the water. I should have listened to you then, but I didn't, and I'm sorry. I promise I will listen to you from now on. If you just give me a chance."

Her mind had been in a completely different spot than their fight in the park, and she had to stop to catch up to him. She blinked in the wind and the drizzle of rain and tried to see her husband more clearly in the muted dark of the night.

"All right," she said, because the things he had said were the things she had been trying to tell him, but just then, she could not say more. She would say more later when they were on land and safe and not likely to be killed, by pirates or otherwise. "I know what laugh means," she said, her voice just as breathy as when she first started speaking, having gained no further confidence from Alec's words, still stunned by his words as she had pulled herself through the hatch in the deck.

But Alec's face folded into confusion, and she realized that what she had said was not a real sentence. She shook her head, trying to find herself deep within her own confusion.

"I'm sorry, Alec. I'm not saying this right. I know it was you, Alec," she said, looking back up at him. "It was you that night in the gardens. You were trying to make me feel better by making me laugh only I—"

She stopped, raising her fingers to his face, realizing she was shaking even as she did so.

Alec smiled, raising his own hand to take her shaking one back into the cocoon of his.

"You walloped me a good one, love," he had stepped closer, his head bent. "I hope you will not do that again if I tell you I love you."

"I love you, too," she whispered even though that was not quite what he had said.

Someone cleared his throat.

"As much as I appreciate this show of affection after four bloody years of watching you two tear each other apart, this is not our ship, and it would be best if we were to leave."

Sarah turned to look at Nathan.

"That's not really your color," she said, pointing to his pirate garb.

Nathan only raised his eyebrows at her.

"Are you all right, Sarah?" Alec said, and she turned to look back at him.

"Quite. How are we going to go about getting off this ship?"

Alec looked up at the grappling lines even as she looked down at her tattered skirts.

"I suppose propriety is no longer a concern, is it?" she said, looking up at him.

"Afraid not, love," he said, and she watched the wicked glint return to his green eyes.

"Would you be so kind as to help me with my skirts, my lord?" she said, turning her back towards him.

"It would be my pleasure, my lady."

He quickly bent over and once more pulled the back of her skirt through the front of her dress, capturing the ruined fabric in a sack.

"As lovely as that scarf is, dear brother, would you mind lending it toward a worthy cause?"

Alec pointed toward the elaborately tied scarf of magnificent crimson around Nathan's neck.

"It will ruin my pirate outfit," he said but obligingly took it off.

Alec wrapped it about her waist, capturing the folds of

cloth until she was free to move without the encumbrance of skirts.

"Did you climb trees as a lass?" he asked.

She shook her head. "No, but I did catch rides on hackneys unseen."

Alec raised an eyebrow. "How you were able to do that is something I wish to know more of. Perhaps, it is a topic for later discussion?"

"Perhaps."

This time Nathan audibly groaned. "Could we please get off the ship today?" he asked, gesturing toward the grappling lines.

Alec grabbed her about the waist. "Are you ready, love? I'll be right behind you."

Sarah nodded and reached for the line.

She had seen the way the men had moved their hands along the rope, one after the other, using one foot to hold the rope as the other closed over top to push the body along. She took a moment to allow her breath to settle, her mind to focus, to concentrate on the swing of the rope as the ship rocked. And then she reached with one hand as her feet slid along the rope. When the deck fell away behind her, she kept her eyes riveted to the ship across the span of water, noticed the darkness of the wood.

"Almost there, love."

Alec's voice was closer than she had expected, and the sound of it sent a jolt of courage through her. She looked to her side and saw him hanging just as she was on the grappling line next to hers.

"Alec, can you promise me something?" she called back.

"Anything."

"I would very much like a bath after this."

She heard Alec's chuckle across the wind.

"Of course, my lady. You may have a bath."

When the ship came into view beneath her, she felt a slight giving of the fear that had gripped her in silence since she had grabbed the grappling line. Hands reached for her and helped her down from the line. As soon as her feet touched the deck, she spun back to the railing, watching as other men helped Alec off of his line.

And then she was in his arms, and he held her with such strength and gentleness that she feared she would cry from the simple joy of it.

"Thank you for not leaving me," she said, a distinct catch in her voice.

"I could never leave you," he said, and his words sent a shiver through her that no touch ever could.

"Promise," she said.

"I promise."

"When did this happen?"

Sarah's head snapped up, and she looked over her shoulder. "Nora?"

She blinked, not believing that the infallible Miss Quinton could be standing before her. Nora turned toward her as she had asked the question of Nathan, who appeared to have just come on board himself

"Yes, my lady?" Nora said, bowing to her.

It was then that Sarah saw that Nora was dressed as a sailor in trousers and jacket.

"Nora!" Sarah said, the shock sounding in her voice. "Are those comfortable?"

Nora grinned. "Extremely. I would advise you to try it sometime."

"Do not get any ideas, Lady Stryden," Alec said from over her head.

"Perhaps just once."

"Perhaps never," he said, moving slightly to bow to Nora.

"Miss Quinton, it's a pleasure to see you again."

179

"Ah, that's Mrs. Black, actually," Nathan said, looking down at Nora.

Alec stopped mid-bow, and Sarah felt her eyebrows shoot up to her hairline.

"Mrs. Black?" Sarah asked and turned to her half-bent husband. "When did this happen?"

Alec straightened and shook his head. "How would I know? I've been with you the whole time."

"Would you two mind going below decks now? It is you these Frenchies are after."

Reginald Davis appeared between them as he made his way toward the quarterdeck and the wheel.

"Prepare to shove off," he called, and Sarah looked up to see sailors high in the riggings, moving like spiders across a web.

"A bath," she said as Alec led her below.

"A bath," he said, "But first we need to make it to shore."

* * *

ALEC COULD FINALLY MOVE AGAIN.

When he had realized they were being rescued, something in him had frozen, stuck on a single idea, a single thought that would not jar loose in his mind.

He just needed to get to Sarah.

And now that she was here, standing in his arms, he could finally function like the trained spy he was. Keeping his arm about Sarah's shoulders, he moved to the staircase leading up to the quarterdeck. He followed in Davis's path to the bridge, bringing Sarah inside with him. The wind still brewed even though the storm seemed to have blown itself out, and he wanted Sarah to be protected at least for a bit from the elements. Once inside the bridge, he helped Sarah remove the make shift belt and return her skirts to their proper place along her legs. He could admit that he had taken slightly longer than necessary to get the nearly destroyed fabric back into place if only to give him a few more minutes of admiring his wife's shapely legs. There would be plenty of time to admire them later, and right now, he had to do whatever Davis told him to do to get them safely back to shore and into the protection of a crowd.

Davis barked orders to his sailors on the bridge. Some scurried below deck while others ran out to the quarterdeck to relay orders to the men in the rigs. Alec watched as the grappling lines were released, the ropes falling away, and the ship that had been their prison drifting into the darkness.

"We didn't get to say goodbye to the captain," Sarah whispered, but he heard the derisive note in her voice.

"Perhaps we'll call on him at some point in the future. When our countries are not at war. What say you?"

Sarah laughed.

It was soft and non-committal, but it was a natural laugh. One pulled out without much thought as to what she was doing.

Everything inside Alec stopped moving, arrested by the sound of that small, weak laugh. He couldn't breathe. He knew he had known how only moments before, but right then, he couldn't have drawn breath if it were the one thing that could get them back to shore.

Sarah finally turned to look at him, and she must have seen something in his face, because a concerned expression spread over her features, and she lifted a hand to cup his cheek.

"You do make me laugh, Alec Black. I've just never let you hear it."

Her words were still whispered, but she could have been shouting for that was how loudly he heard them.

He made his wife laugh.

He had heard it with his own ears, and it was a sound unlike anything he had heard previously. It was magical and light. It was beauty and miracles. It was exactly what he had been waiting to hear for four long years.

"Thank you," he said, although he wasn't sure why he was thanking her. She couldn't possibly understand what her laughter meant to him. And indeed, she frowned.

"I don't know why it's so important to you that I laugh, Alec. Do you think we could talk about that later?"

Alec felt the numbing sensation spread through his body once more. Sarah never spoke about things, at least not to him, and suddenly, it sounded like the most important thing in the world to do just then.

"Perhaps after a bath, my lady," he said, feeling the smile move across his face, watching her returning smile as she gazed up at him.

In the weak lantern light of the bridge on the ship that was meant to save them from the damned French, in the middle of the English Channel with the rocky seas threatening to overturn them at any moment, Alec fell in love with Sarah all over again. And it was the second best moment of his life. Second only, of course, to the first time he had fallen in love with her, in a duke's garden under the light of a midnight moon.

"My lord, are you implying that I am in current need of bathing? How dare you make such an implication to a lady?"

He admired her attempt to sound highbrow when she was covered from head to tattered slippers in salt water and muck. Alec stepped back and gave a gracious bow. "I do beg your pardon, my lady. How uncouth of me to make such a comment about your person."

Sarah laughed, and this time, it was solid and sure, a noise so profound, Alec laughed in return. It wasn't until Sarah was resting peacefully in his arms once more that he realized people were watching them. Nathan and Nora to be exact. Nora stood with the regal and unmoving pose of a trained servant while Nathan rudely stared at them.

"I'm glad to see you two have managed to find a way between your differences," Nathan said.

"I do not think there were any differences between them, Mr. Black," Nora returned, "I think it was just a matter of understanding properly what one was saying to the other. It can be quite difficult you know."

Alec went to nod and then stopped. "About this Mr. Black and Mrs. Black thing, would you care to explain?"

Sarah's head nodded against his shoulder. "I think an explanation would be wonderful."

Nathan shrugged. "There isn't much to explain. You were missing. Sarah ran off after you. We had to try to find you to save you from whatever trouble it was you found yourself in, and in the course of events, we ended up married to one another. Is that about how it went, dear?" He directed the last part to Nora, who nodded.

"Yes, I do believe that quite sums up the matter. Will we be in dock soon? We need to get these two out of these wet clothes or it will be the death of them."

Alec felt a slight bit of reassurance at Nora's motherly tone, but this again stopped him. "Where's Samuel then?"

Nathan smiled. "He's been sent off to Great Aunt Lydia."

Alec felt the blood drain from his face. "Dear God, man, he's going to return with all kinds of bravado notions in his head."

Nora smiled at him. "So I have heard, and I cannot wait to see the outcome."

Sarah moved against him. "And what of Jane and Richard?"

Nathan looked at Nora. "Well, they are on their wedding trip, you see. In the port of Dover."

"And we would be their servants," Nora supplied.

"Quite the ruse then, I see," Alec said, his arm unconsciously tightening around Sarah. "Do we have any cover to keep us from detection once we return to shore?"

Nathan shook his head. "The plan is to generally keep you in a large crowd until we can safely return to London. We will be traveling by ship to Liverpool first as a distraction. We hope to lose anyone that would continue to follow you. We hope this entire ordeal will be enough to convince certain persons that you are not worth kidnapping again."

"I beg to differ on that point, brother. I think I am definitely worth kidnapping," Alec said, mock indignity in his voice.

"I would second that," Sarah said.

Nathan only raised an eyebrow.

"Get ready, laddies and lassies," Davis called over to them. "We'll be making the pier in due course, and then ye'd best get off me ship."

Alec looked at Nathan. "Wherever did he learn to talk like that?"

Nathan shrugged. "Who knows where Davis picks things up?"

The four of them made their way back out to the quarterdeck and down to the level where the gangplank would lead them to the pier. Alec had carefully looked over himself and Sarah. He quickly tied the scarf that they had used as a belt around Sarah's head to give her some level of camouflage, but he had nothing for himself. He looked at Nathan.

"Mind if I borrow your hat, pirate?"

Nathan obliging took the thing off his head. "Nothing would give me more pleasure."

The gangplank lowered, and they were moving even before it hit the treads of the pier.

Even at this late hour, there was activity on the docks, but not the kind of activity that welcomed genteel company. Alec kept his arm around Sarah as they made their way swiftly to the shore road where they could pick up a hackney that would take them away from this docks. Nathan and Nora moved ahead of them, a distinct distance between them as Nora clearly looked every inch a man and somewhat threatening in her authoritative walk. His brother had most certainly gotten himself a remarkable woman.

They gained purchase on the shore road, and the traffic moved swiftly past them, carrying gentlemen to and fro as they made their way from gaming hell to gaming hell and then to brothel. Alec's arm tightened again.

"If you squeeze anymore, I shall shatter," Sarah said, and he loosened his arm immediately.

Out of the flow of traffic, a carriage suddenly appeared before them, and Alec had never been so happy to see the colors of the Duke of Lofton. Nora was opening the door even as Nathan jumped up on the box with the driver. Alec did not hesitate. He swept his wife up into his arms and boarded the carriage. The door shut with a snap, and Alec caught a flash as Nora swung onto the tiger's step at the rear. And then the carriage was moving.

"That must be the best damn housekeeper I have ever met."

Alec looked down at his wife as she sat cradled in his arms, raising his eyebrows at her indelicate words.

"I would have to agree with you, Lady Stryden. I would have to agree with you indeed."

And then he just held her as the carriage raced through the traffic of Dover, taking them away from the things which threatened the happiness they so recently found.

CHAPTER 12

 *over, England*
April 1815

SARAH LAY PERFECTLY STILL on the bed, letting the entire world collapse on her like a wave that ran the length of her body before disappearing from reach. She felt its cool, fleeting touch, but before it could spark worry or fear in her person, it simply disappeared, and she was left feeling nothing at all.

Nothing, except the warm touch of her husband's hand in hers.

When they had arrived at The Owl and Fork Inn, they had entered the establishment through the rear, keeping to the servants' halls and stairs until finding their way up to the suite of rooms reserved by the Duke and Duchess of Lofton for their belated wedding trip. Sarah did not know how she had had the energy to move at all at the point, let alone up so many flights of stairs. With the edge of danger removed, her body had quite simply given up, and now it wanted rest.

But the duke and duchess were awake and alert when they had entered the chamber and had immediately started asking questions. Sarah could remember very little of the entire thing as Alec did the talking, and she stood there, trying desperately not to fall asleep. Baths were ordered for both of them, and then Nora was helping her out of the remains of her dress.

It was just she and Nora, alone together in the room set aside for Alec and Sarah upon their rescue. A fire roared in the fireplace even though it was the middle of the night. And between the warmth of the flames and the heat of the bathwater, Sarah knew she was going to fall asleep.

She remembered reaching out to Nora, telling her to stay, to keep her awake. And she had.

Nora sat on a stool by the fire, working her way around Sarah's gown as if determining if the garment could be salvaged. Sarah had more gowns than she would ever wear in a lifetime and knew this one would not be missed. But she also knew that Nora came from an entirely different background than she, and that saving any garment was a priority. So she kept her mouth shut and listened to Nora tell her about what had happened after Sarah had run off after Alec and they both got themselves kidnapped.

She listened to how Nora and Nathan had been wed under the pressure of discovery and how Samuel had discovered what had happened to Lord Archer, the man Nathan had been assigned to assassinate because of his treasonous acts for the French.

And she listened when Nora told her how she had shot and killed the man who had raped her so many years ago. It was at this story that Sarah had become fully awake, sitting in now tepid bath water, the aches in her body receding with every word Nora said.

And then Nora was fetching a nightgown and robe for

her, and before she could protest, Nora had her tucked in bed, the covers a comforting weight on her bruised body.

She had almost been asleep when the soft click of a door knob turning told her her husband had entered their room. She had been wondering where he was in some lost corner of her mind, but the tired ache of her body trumped any other thought, and she had only been concentrating on sleeping. But then the bed dipped with his weight, and she rolled slightly toward him. His hand found hers, and they lay that way for several moments before he finally spoke.

"You hit him with a water jug?"

Sarah forced her eyelids to open. It would not do to fall asleep on Alec after they had so recently come to a sort of truce between them, a truce that was quickly leading to better understanding. Sarah had never even imagined that their discord was a simple case of misunderstanding, but then, she most likely had never given enough due to proper communication. She rather thought yelling at a person solved all matters, but even she could be proven wrong.

"I did," she said.

"Where did you get a water jug?"

Sarah thought back to the old man who had helped her, who led her through the dark passages of their prison to the hatch that would gain her freedom and bring her back to Alec.

"A friend," she said. "What were you doing scampering about in the middle of the Duke of Kent's gardens that night? I know why I was out of bed, but what were you doing out of bed? Surely, your father and Jane didn't know what you were about."

She heard Alec turn his head on the pillow beside her.

"I was going to meet a girl," he said without hesitation, and Sarah turned her own head to look at him.

"A girl? Truly?"

Alec smiled in the dark of the room, the warm glow from the fire casting shadows across his face. "A very pretty girl. But then I ran into you and got most distracted."

"Why did you help me that night? I could have taken care of myself."

Alec shrugged under the weight of their many covers. "I liked you. I remembered you from earlier in the day when we children had been assigned the task of playing croquet with the nannies and being told to enjoy it. I recalled that you struck the balls as hard as you possibly could and smiled rather mischievously when they toppled into the pond."

Sarah smiled at the memory of it. "I was most bored," she said, as if that would justify it.

"I was, too, but I was not brave enough to demonstrate it the way you did."

"Do you think that was impolite of me?"

Alec shook his head. "I think certain things are expected of people born in certain places at certain times, but no one considers the fact that we're all just humans. And sometimes, we would like to be left to do what we wish to do."

"What do you mean?" she asked, and even she marveled at the fact that she had just asked her husband to explain himself further when in the past, she would have called him an uncomplimentary name and changed the subject.

She knew Alec noticed it, too, when he raised his eyebrows at her in the near dark.

"I mean that class isn't really anything other than a label applied to a person. The label is worthless if the intrinsic qualities of the person are found lacking."

Sarah felt her mouth fall open. "That must be the most intelligent thing I have ever heard you say, Alec Black."

Alec laughed softly. "It's hard to sound intelligent when a person is focused on making another person laugh."

Sarah wanted to ask something about that, but Alec kept going.

"Sometimes society can be harsh, Sarah, but it truly is not worth getting your nose bent about it. Who cares what an old biddy has to say about the color of your skirts if she herself has never said a kind word to anyone in her lifetime? I would rather not care for such a person's opinions. What was it you were saying about dodging carriages and what not as a child? I think that stuff speaks volumes to a person's character and not so much a person's luck on being born into the right family. Luck doesn't require courage or bravery or intelligence. How can luck be the judge of anything?"

Sarah did not speak.

She let her husband's words wash over her, the wave returning once more, only this time it was gentle and serene and its weight barely noticeable. His words were a caress, consumed by such a level of love and understanding that Sarah had not witnessed the like of it before. But she had to be sure. She had to be certain before she allowed the caress to lure her into hope.

"Alec, are you saying that you do not care if I am a bastard?"

Alec looked at her, his gaze unwavering. "Sarah, I believe there is a very important part of my life that you have failed to take note of. Have you met my brother, Nathan?"

Sarah blinked at him. "Of course, I have met Nathan—"

She stopped speaking, feeling her eyes grow round. "Oh, Alec. I am a complete idiot," she whispered, and he laughed softly again, the noise a musical sound in her ears.

"Oh, come now, love, I wouldn't be quite so harsh. You are not a complete idiot, but perhaps you missed a thing or two."

"But Alec," she said, coming up on an elbow to lean over him. "Your brother is a bastard. His mother...your father...he..." She couldn't get the right words in the right order.

"Yes, our father and his mother were not wed when Nathan was conceived and born, and I could not have asked for a better brother."

"So you do not care that I am..." She couldn't find the word.

"I do not care about any of that, Sarah, but I am most interested in how you managed to secure clandestine rides on carriages without being caught. That topic requires much greater detail from the source, I believe."

Sarah matched his smile and lowered herself back down to the pillows. "A lady never tells her secrets, my lord," she said and did not flinch when she referred to herself as a lady.

"Not even to her husband?"

"Not even," she said, smiling at him in the dark. "But there is something you could tell me. Why is it so important that you make me laugh?"

Alec's smile faded, and he turned away from her.

But Sarah was already moving, bringing her hand up to his face and drawing him back to her. "We are no longer playing this game, Stryden. I talk and you listen. You talk and I listen. No more hiding, and no more misunderstanding."

Alec looked at her. "When did you become such a demanding shrew?"

"When you taught me how," she said. "Now do not change the subject. Why must you make me laugh?"

She thought he would evade the question again, but it appeared he was merely thinking how to word his response.

"It's a very long story, Sarah."

She nodded. "And where else do I have to be at this moment exactly?"

"You should be sleeping, getting the rest your body truly needs."

Sarah shook her head. "I'll hear this story first, and then I'll sleep."

"Demanding," he muttered, but then he took a breath to tell her what he meant. "Nathan was born exactly three years before me, almost to the day. No one has ever told me what happened to his mother, but I can only imagine she either died shortly after giving birth to him or she simply did not want him. Whatever the circumstances, our father did want him, and he did everything he could to make sure Nathan was legally his. And then Nathan came to live with him, and he realized he was completely not prepared for a child. But he loved Nathan. I remember him telling Jane about Nathan as a baby, the sounds he would make in his sleep and the stories he would tell when he was just learning to speak."

Their hands had become entwined between them, and Sarah squeezed his hand now.

"You must have listened at your father's door a lot after you thought you killed Nathan."

Alec smiled. "I did. It's very traumatic thinking you killed your brother. I needed all of the comfort I could get."

Sarah raised her head enough to kiss her husband softly on the lips. "Please continue," she said.

"And that was when our father realized he needed to beget a legal heir. Having Nathan in his keep made something in him snap, and any desire he had had in being a rogue and whatever other terms were in vogue in those days for calling a man a rake simply vanished. He was ready to assume his responsibility to the title. So he wed my mother. Nathan has told me that it was not a love match, but a match of sincere respect. He had heard stories from his nanny of what the two of them had been like during the courtship as whomever the Duke of Lofton chose to wed, she would need to accept Nathan as a part of their lives. And my mother did."

"What was her name?" Sarah interrupted, needing to

know just then the name of this woman who had left such a mark on her son.

"Emily," Alec said, his eyes going distant as the name left his lips. "Her name was Emily."

Sarah tightened her grip on his hand. "Go on," she said softly.

"They were wed, and I was born a short year later, four days after Nathan's third birthday. And Emily died five days after Nathan's third birthday."

The last of his words came out as barely a whisper with such guttural agony held in them that Sarah was surprised he had managed the words at all. She reached up and laid a hand along his cheek.

"And that is the first real thing that I can remember," he said, "I remember killing my mother."

Tears came to Alec's eyes as he slipped into his memories and away from her.

"Alec," she said rather harshly, but his eyes cleared almost instantly, "Stop being ridiculous."

He looked at her then, his eyes focused and a little surprised.

She smiled. "I was just trying to get your attention," she said, "And now that I have it, you need to explain to me. Why do you think you killed your mother? Did someone tell you that you did?"

Alec shook his head against her hand. "No one had to tell me. I just knew. I knew I had killed her, and there was nothing I could to make up for it."

"Why would you have to make up for it, Alec?"

She saw him swallow, heard the sound of it through the darkness of the room.

"I had to make up for it so my father would love me."

Tears came to his eyes again, and she held onto him, one hand squeezing his while the other worked its way into the hair at the nape of his neck, drawing him closer to her.

"What do you mean, Alec? Your father does love you."

Alec nodded, even as the tears held in his eyes. "I had to make him laugh," he said, and realization spread through Sarah in a cold shiver.

"Alec, did you make your father laugh so he would love you?"

The words brought forward the image of Alec as a little boy, struggling every day to make his father laugh because of some misguided idea that by making him laugh, his father would love him and forgive him for killing his mother.

"Yes," he said then, and his eyes closed as the tears ran down his cheeks.

Sarah stared at her husband, the ever ridiculous and jovial Alec Black who now cried in her arms.

So Sarah slapped him.

Alec's eyes flew open, perfectly clear of tears, and his mouth hung slightly open. "Did you just hit me?" he asked.

Sarah nodded. "I did, and I'm sorry, but you're being ridiculous, and I am not very good with this discussion thing yet, so I got your attention the only way I know how, which is to cause you physical harm."

Alec only stared at her, so she sat up again, leaning on an elbow to make sure he understood how serious she was.

"Alec, you cannot in any sense of the matter be responsible for killing your mother. You were a baby, and most likely, your mother did everything she could to make sure you lived. Did you ever think of that?"

Alec blinked, and she knew he hadn't.

"Your mother probably tried desperately to make sure you were born, and you have spent your entire life trying to make people love you by making them laugh because you feel some sort of guilt at her death?"

She paused.

"Alec Black, you are a complete idiot."

She finished with an exasperated sigh and let her words sink in. But Alec sat up much too quickly, drawing her with him.

"What are you saying?" he asked, holding onto her arm as he pulled her close to him.

Sarah shrugged under his grasp. "You should talk to your father, Alec. He's the one that you've been trying to make love you. He would be the only one to tell you whether or not your efforts have been misguided."

Alec didn't say anything, so she plunged on.

"You had to talk to me, didn't you? To find out where we misunderstood one another. Why not speak with your father?"

Alec still did not speak, and Sarah pulled on the arm that held onto her.

"Alec? What are you thinking? I cannot read your mind."

"You think talking to my father about this is truly necessary?" he finally asked.

Sarah nodded. "I loved you even without you making me laugh, so I think it is very important to speak with your father."

She laid a hand on his chest, felt the beat of his heart against her palm.

"There is a lot of guilt that you are carrying in here, Alec. Guilt that may be unfounded. Ask your father. Find out the truth."

Alec did not say anything. He simply gathered her into his arms and lay back against the pillows, her head falling to the space below his chin. She settled in, feeling the pulse of his heart beneath her ear.

"I will speak with him in the morning," she heard her husband say somewhere above her head.

She nodded. "Hold me until then, Alec. Please."

"Always," he whispered, and she let sleep find her.

* * *

DAWN RADIATED its colors across the sky when Alec woke his wife with an ardent kiss, searing her lips with all of the desire pent up inside him. His hands were slow and deliberate, moving across her with an intent so natural and basic that his mind focused on everything else. It focused on the taste of her lips, the sounds she made in her throat when he touched her just there, and the feel of her leg as it came to wrap around his.

He helped her from her nightgown, tossing the garment to the floor, as his hands savored the feel of her bare skin. He took a moment to just feel her, feel her supple and lush body move against his, length to length. The brush of her breasts along his chest, the sweep of her hands up his back, the pulse of her heartbeat against his lips as he nipped kisses down her throat.

For four years he had waited for this very moment. The moment when he could savor his wife, every last inch of her.

This was not about the carnal act itself. This was a learning thing, a desiring thing. It was something with weight and dimension that he could not begin to know or understand but that he looked forward to studying every day for the rest of his life and still not know the answers. This was Sarah, and she finally let him in, into her and into them. This was what they were as husband and wife. And although some priest had long ago spoken words that would unite them forever, it wasn't until this moment that Alec could attest to the fact that those words were spoken in truth. That now Sarah truly was his wife and he, her husband. Only now did they understand each other enough to become one.

His fingers skimmed the sensitive pocket at the back of her knees as his mouth captured her moan of pleasure, the vocalization of what his touch did to her. The sound of it drove him forward faster, made him dare to explore farther. He traced the line of her thigh as it moved into the sensual curve of her hip.

He slipped a leg between hers and let his thigh come to rest at her apex, felt the heat that resonated there. She whimpered then, and he opened his eyes to watch her, to see the pleasure as if it were a physical thing that could be observed. She was stunning in her ecstasy. Her thick golden hair spread across the linen of the pillow, framing her delicate face. Her cheeks were flush with desire. The desire he had put there, and he leaned down to kiss her, to drive her closer to the edge.

He felt it when her hips began to move, when she began to rub herself against him. He broke the kiss to look down to the place where their bodies met, where her hips moved against him, grinding into his thigh. The sight of it sent a surge of lust through him so intense it took his breath away. He captured her mouth once more, pushing his tongue inside to taste her, to take all of her senses. He wanted her to know it was him, that it was Alec that made her feel this way.

But it wasn't enough. He had to know her completely. He had to make her feel all of him. Completely.

"Sarah," he coaxed her, watching her eyelids flutter open, her gaze settling on his. "I need you to tell me if I do something that you don't like or that frightens you," he said and watched her eyes grow into dark pools of desire.

"I just want you, Alec," she whispered, and he came to her.

His mouth closed on hers as his hands settled around her hips. He broke the kiss even as he flipped her over. She made a soft noise of surprise as she came to rest on her stomach. Alec knelt, taking in the beauty in the slant of her back. With a single fingertip, he traced the curve of it from the nape of her neck to the sensitive spot at the very verge of her buttocks. He heard her sharp intake of breath as his finger left her skin. He leaned down, licking gently where his finger had been. He felt her twitch, heard her attempt to cover the whimper his touch drew from her. She squirmed beneath him, and he grasped her hips, holding her still. And then he ran his tongue up the length of her spine. She pulled against him, and he knew the torture he caused her by holding her still. But feeling her vibrate beneath, hearing her aborted whimpers, sent spikes of undulating desire through him.

His erection was hard, throbbing, and as he moved up the length of her, it came to rest in the nestle of her buttocks. He rubbed it against her, and this time she did not try to stop the moan that erupted in her throat.

"Alec, please," she whispered, but he only kissed the nape of her neck, coiling her long golden hair in his hand as he moved it out of his way.

He suckled and nibbled, and she bucked underneath him. The movement had her rubbing against him, and now he was the one who moaned. The sensation shocked him, having never felt something so powerful, so demanding, so right. He settled between her legs, prodding ever so slightly at her apex. She made a noise, and before he knew what she was about, she came up on her knees.

"Please, Alec," she said, her voice thick with desire.

Her succulent cheeks came into his hands as she changed positions, and his throbbing shaft rested at her very core, flexing in the heat of her. He couldn't stop himself. He plunged into her from behind, his hands gripping her to go deeper, to fill her more fully. She cried out, and he felt her tight, hot sheath close around him. He went so incredibly deep that he worried he hurt her. But she started to move, her hips slamming against him as if to take him even deeper.

He moved with her until her climax gripped him, pulsating in a wave of sheer pleasure as she collapsed into the pillows.

He heard her labored breathing, felt the last of her climax spasm around him, and he gritted his teeth to hold on. He wanted to watch her face when he came inside of her. He pulled out and carefully turned her over. Her skin was flush with want, and her mouth hung open as she tried to draw in air. He stayed that way for a moment, kneeling between her spread legs as he drank in the sight of her. Her slightly rounded stomach, her small, upright breasts, and her silky ivory thighs.

He ran his hands down her skin, watching the gooseflesh appear in the wake of his touch. Her legs fell farther apart, spreading her center to him. His gaze riveted to the pink flesh of her intimate folds, unable to look away. They pulsed with the remains of her orgasm, and Alec bent, putting his lips to the soft skin.

Sarah cried out, her hands gripping the back of his head. He felt her nails find purchase, and he shivered as she drew her fingers along his scalp.

"Alec," she hissed, and he heard the utter lust in her voice.

So he slipped his tongue into her. She moaned, a sound so guttural and basic he would have looked up to make sure it was still his wife, but he couldn't have moved then if the fires of Hell burned at his feet. He sipped at her, stroking her with his tongue. He moved back, tracing the folds of her core, moving farther still to bite at the delicate crease of her thigh. When his teeth connected with her skin, she reared up off the bed, her hands gripping his head so hard he thought his skull would shatter. But as soon as she sat up, she fell backwards, a weak moan slipping between her lips. When his mouth moved back to her most sensitive nub, he knew he would send her over the edge. Again.

Her next moan came from deep in her throat, moving up

and outward in an exhale of simple desire, and her hips shuddered against his mouth. He couldn't take more and moved up, coming to rest between her opened legs. The taste of her was still on his lips when he slipped inside of her with ease. The noise she made then was one he would never forget. It was soft, like the caress of a lover, but so distinct his ears rang with the sound of it.

He cradled her head in his hands.

"Look at me, Sarah," he whispered, and her eyes fluttered open.

She reached up and wrapped her small hands around his wrists.

"I love you," he said and began to move within her.

He rocked against her, and her eyes closed as he felt her muscles tighten around him. She was small, stretching perfectly around him, and he gritted his teeth, holding onto control for as long as he could, not wanting the moment to end. He ran short kisses along her collarbones and up along the line of her neck, coming to rest in the fragile spot behind her ear. He couldn't seem to stop, so he flicked out his tongue and smiled at the whimper that came from his wife's lips.

"Alec," she said, more breath than actual word, but he knew what she meant. He knew what she felt even as he felt it himself. Knew what she wanted, what she needed even as he knew he needed and wanted it himself. He drove into her, and her legs suddenly wrapped around his waist, pulling him into her.

It sent him deliriously close to the edge, and he reigned back, wanting to prolong this, the first of many times he would truly make love to his wife. But the feeling was too intense, too strong, and even he could not control it.

"Sarah," he whispered.

"Come with me," she said, and he exploded as the first ripples of her orgasm closed around him.

He floated on it, floated on the release that consumed him, and he wasn't even sure if he was conscious enough to make certain he did not crush his wife. He finally rolled off of her, feeling the weight of the moment as he finally surfaced from the desire induced fog that had lain over them.

Sarah was in his arms, her head resting on his shoulder as her hand cupped the side of his neck as if holding him closer were possible. He doubted they could have been any closer if they tried, but the feeling of his wife's grip on him left him motionless in her embrace.

"I love you, Alec," she whispered.

"I love you, too," he whispered back.

He blinked at the ceiling above them, at the way the morning sun moved across it, pushing ever deeper into the room. Soon they would need to get up, get ready to move again, to board a ship that would take them to Liverpool and hopefully to safety. And once they returned to London, the rest of their lives would begin.

"Sarah?" he asked and felt more than heard her response in a quiet hum against his neck.

"That day in the park. When you said you would talk to the War Office. That you would arrange everything. That you wouldn't be a burden to me anymore. Do you still mean that?"

He didn't know how much her words had affected him until lying there, completely sated from making extraordinary love to his wife, he realized how painful it would be for her to leave him. Physical pain with a realness so sharp it could possibly kill him.

Sarah moved against him, coming up on one elbow. The hand that had been holding onto his neck moved lower, playing in the hairs on his chest. Her hair stuck up in odd places, and a very satisfied smile graced her lips.

"If you were to repeat what it was that you just did to me, my lord, I shan't mean a single word of it."

A smile came unbidden to his lips. Whether it was at her words or at the sight of her, so well loved, he could not be sure.

"Is that a challenge, lady wife?"

Her smile deepened even as an edge of playful lust came to it, and he suddenly realized his wife was playing at seduction.

"That depends, my lord."

"Depends on what?"

"On whether or not you are up to such a feat. I have heard gentlemen of the peerage can be such dandies."

Alec moved so quickly, a look of surprise flashed in her eyes before she could cover it with a lazy gaze down the length of his body. He pinned her beneath him, settling between her now spread legs.

"Oh, I do believe I am up for that challenge. Let's pray that you can survive the outcome."

Sarah's laugh cascaded through the room, and Alec waited a moment, soaking in the pleasure the simple sound of her laugh gave him, before he kissed her again.

CHAPTER 13

*A*lec entered the common room of their suite in The Owl and Fork Inn to find his father seated at the table by the bank of windows along the far wall, the Times spread out in front of him. The sun was to his back, casting the older man in shadow, and Alec moved forward with an unfamiliar touch of trepidation. A serving cart sat next to the table, and Alec's stomach grumbled at the sight of it.

The Duke of Lofton looked up, a smile coming to his features, a face so familiar to Alec.

"Good morning, my boy. Why, you do not look any worse for the wear, do you?" his father said, as he stood and came toward him.

Alec wasn't sure what his father would do. The man had not been demonstrably affectionate since Alec had surrendered his last pair of knee pants to his nanny. It wasn't that Richard was not affectionate at all. He had just respected the wishes of his growing sons to be men in all ways, including signs of affection. But then, in the middle of a suite in The Owl and Fork in the port of Dover, Richard Lofton embraced his son.

And Alec hugged his father back.

He felt the surge of love in his father's arms, the same arms that had held him when he realized he had not killed Nathan, the same arms that had held him whenever a nightmare had threatened his sleep, the same arms that now told him his father had been worried about him.

"I'm all right, Father," he said then, his voice muffled as his face connected with the top of his father's shoulder.

Richard did not loosen his grip for a moment, and Alec could not say more.

"You'll have some breakfast then," Richard said, letting Alec go with a thump on the back. He moved away toward the table and with a flourish of his hand indicated the spread laid out. "There are eggs and kippers and more eggs..." his voice trailed off.

Alec took one of the chairs and reached for the tea pot. "I would love some eggs and well, eggs."

Richard resumed his seat.

"Where is Nathan?"

"Reconnaissance mission," Richard said, reaching for a plate of eggs to hand to Alec. "Thatcher and Lady Cavanaugh are still unaccounted for."

Alec looked up from piling eggs onto his plate. "Unaccounted for?"

"Yes." Richard picked up his tea cup. "They were to follow your captors after the exchange took place. The War Office needs to know if they are in allegiance with the French or if they were simply acting as paid liaisons. Thatcher was hired to do just that with the assistance of Lady Cavanaugh. They followed the men through the wharf last night, but Nathan lost track of them. He's gone down to the docks this morning to see if he can learn anything new."

Alec swallowed a bit of egg. "Captain Teyssier, the Frenchman in charge on the ship where Nathan rescued us.

He came into possession of Thatcher's hat. I do not know where or by what means he secured it, but something most certainly happened to Thatcher last evening."

Richard looked concerned. "Do you think he's been captured, too? I grow tired of all of these rescue missions."

Alec chuckled.

"No, Father, I do not believe he has been captured. The French captain said he fled with a rather remarkable lady."

"I have heard Lady Cavanaugh called many things, but remarkable has never been one of them," Richard said.

Alec helped himself to some toast. Thinking he may not get a chance to be alone with his father in the near future if they were all to be soon aboard a vessel bound for Liverpool, Alec quickly changed the subject. "Father, can you tell me about my mother? Can you tell me about Emily?"

Richard's face was blank. Alec could not see a single emotion come across it.

"What has brought this on?" Richard finally said, leaning back in his chair, his face contracting into a look of concern, an emotion that Alec could see clearly and feel just as clearly.

"It was just—"

He didn't know what he had planned to say, but sitting there, staring at his father, all of the thoughts in his head simply vanished. "I didn't mean to kill her," he finally said, and the words shocked even him as they sounded harsh and bald in the silence of the room.

"What makes you think you killed her?" his father asked, his tone impassive.

"It's my fault she's dead. If she hadn't given birth to me—"

"She would have died just as easily by the common sniffles."

Alec stopped talking, his tongue growing large in his mouth. He swallowed. "I beg your pardon?"

Richard took a sip of his tea and set his cup down in its

saucer. "Emily Higgins was a frail girl. I can remember how small her wrists were. Reminded me over much of a bird, and I thought any single pebble from a careless child's sling-shot could fell her. But she surprised both of us when she gave birth to you."

Alec shook his head. "I don't understand. Mother was frail?"

Richard nodded. "Very. When I married her, my mother was concerned she'd never be able to carry a child to term, but it was difficult, you see. With Nathan. A woman was not going to accept her husband's mistakes so easily. But Emily did. Emily never treated Nathan any differently. To her, he was just a child, a child deserving of her love. And so I married her, and we hoped for the best. She became pregnant almost immediately. The doctor ordered bed rest by her fifth month. She took it very seriously. She used to sing to you, you know."

Richard took another sip of tea while Alec stared at him. His mother sang to him in the womb?

"It's one of the memories of her that I cherish from the short time I had with her. She sang beautifully. It was almost haunting. Nathan would often sneak out of the nursery and into her rooms just to listen. She would let him stay, of course, and that's how I would find the three of you. Emily holding you with a hand to her belly, Nathan asleep at her side."

Alec saw it in his mind, his mother, full with pregnancy, and a sleeping young Nathan at her side.

"What happened?" Alec asked, not surprised by the strain in his voice.

"It came time for you to be born, and she became ill. The doctor called it toxemia. We were prepared for it, and Emily had made me swear when we first learned she was with child that no matter what happened, we would save the baby first.

Your mother loved you, Alec, even though she had never met you."

Alec absorbed the statement like balm. The words like medicine coated him, and he felt a deep ache that he had carried with him for as long as he could remember begin to heal.

"She wanted to save me?" Alec asked.

"Of course," Richard said, pressing his fingertips together and apart in his lap, "There was to be no question of it. When the doctor realized her blood was full of toxins, he had to decide if he would allow the birth to continue as it would or if he would try to hasten delivery, which surely would have killed your mother but would most likely have saved you. Emily told him to hasten the delivery."

The words hit Alec with the force of Sarah's right cross. It had him sitting up in his chair, his breakfast forgotten. "She told him to hasten the delivery?"

Richard nodded. "Yes, Alec. It was your mother's decision to put herself into peril if it meant saving you. And she chose to save you."

Alec could not find anything to say. Years of guilt weighing down his shoulders suddenly lifted, and air rushed into his lungs with speed and alacrity. But following the rush of air came the quick feeling of an all-encompassing love, something much greater than that which even his father had given to him as a child and still did. This was the insurmountable love of a mother protecting her child, and his mother had shown him that love in the greatest way possible.

"I didn't kill her," he finally whispered, but the words held no meaning for him. The agony he had carried was gone, and in its place, love reigned, radiating a warmth and joy he had never felt before in his life.

Richard shook his head.

"You did not kill her, son. She loved you, and she gave her

life for you. I will love her until the day I die for that, because I could not have asked for a better son and heir."

Alec stared at his father. "What do you mean?" he asked.

Richard laughed. "What is it that you don't understand, Alec?" he said, his laugh still lingering in his voice. "You have made me so proud, and I am honored that you will take the title of the Duke of Lofton one day. Your mother would be proud of you as well. And if the rumor is true that you have worked out that nonsense with Sarah, she would be even more proud. There isn't a woman around who can match Sarah for her intelligence and strength. It's a fine lady you've wed, Alec, and it would suit you to keep her happy."

"I plan to do so, Father," he said, feeling a smile return to his face. He picked up his fork again, having remembered his breakfast. "Are you certain I am fit for the title? You do have another son, you know."

Richard rolled his eyes, picking up the forgotten Times.

"One that gives me constant reasons to worry for his well-being."

"Why do I sense that statement is about me?"

Alec turned toward the door as Nathan entered, his greatcoat swinging as he moved. Alec gestured toward the spread.

"You'd better eat up. I'm starving, and I do not promise to save you any."

He had carried the guilt of his mother's death for the whole of his life, and in a single instant, the weight had vanished. Alec felt light and free and hopeful. He felt hopeful about the future. About his life. About his life with Sarah. About everything.

Nathan shed his greatcoat, taking a place at the table. "Do I dare ask where the ladies are?"

"Only if I may ask how it is that you find yourself married, brother," Alec said, forking some kippers into his mouth. "Because last I checked, you were most certainly a bachelor." Here he turned to his father. "And whose idea was it to send Samuel to Great Aunt Lydia? The child's going to return with all kinds of ideas."

"I always take the opportunity to blame Jane when I can, so I will do so now," Richard said from behind his paper.

His sons only smiled.

"What did you learn of Thatcher?" Alec said, reaching to refill his tea.

Nathan spoke around a mouthful of egg. "Unfortunately, not good news. It appears Thatcher and the good Lady Cavanaugh boarded a ship last night."

Richard set down his paper. "A ship? But wherever were they going?"

Nathan shrugged and swallowed. "I believe they were attempting pursuit of the gold-toothed fiend."

Alec laughed. "Is that what you are calling him?"

"Does he have a name?" Richard countered.

Alec nodded. "Sven. At least, that was the name he gave us."

Richard looked to Nathan, but Nathan shook his head.

"The only intelligence on the subject is that his name is Loyal Bentons."

Alec laughed. "Well, that is what I would call ironic."

Richard frowned. "It sounds like a hired job."

Alec nodded in agreement. "I would have to support that conclusion. It sounded as if he was being paid a handsome sum of money to bring my person to Dover. I don't think he would be the type to do anything out of loyalty to a cause despite his name."

"Do we know which ship they boarded and where that ship was bound?" Richard asked, but Nathan was already shaking his head.

"My contact couldn't be sure which ship they ended up

on. They are either on their way to the Americas or..." his voice trailed off.

Richard and Alec both looked at him.

"Or they are headed to Italy," he finally finished.

"Italy?" Richard and Alec said at the same time.

"God help us all," Richard muttered.

"Isn't Napoleon's brother-in-law or some sort still in charge of Italy?" Alec asked, looking to his father.

Richard shrugged. "As far as I know they allowed him to return."

"Italy would not be the best choice of destinations then," Alec said. "But perhaps the Americas. Are those American chaps still trying to take Canada?"

Nathan shook his head.

"No, I think they're done going on about that."

Alec shook his head.

"I don't see what they're all about. They already took the Colonies. Why is that they feel they must own everything?"

"Said the British gentleman," Nathan added, and Alec laughed.

Richard made a noise of agreement and went back to his paper.

"So, Nathan, tell me. How are you finding the married life?"

* * *

NORA STOOD behind her as she plaited her hair into a tight braid that she would then loop into a circle at the base of Sarah's neck. It was lucky for both she and Lady Lofton that Nora had paid attention when the lady's maids of the various houses she had been employed in had carried on when it came to styling said mistress's hair. Otherwise, this ruse of servants accompanying their masters on a wedding trip would never have passed the first whisper of suspicion.

Sarah kept still while Nora worked the last of the plait.

"I still don't understand how the men with the gold teeth work into this entire ordeal."

"Man. There was only one gentleman with gold teeth," Sarah corrected Jane, who lounged on the settee by the window of Sarah and Alec's room in the suite at The Owl and Fork Inn.

"And gold teeth? How gaudy," Jane said with enough emphasis that no one could mistake her opinion on the subject.

Sarah watched Nora in the mirror of the dressing table as the braid she had been working on went into place. The style was unlike any Sarah had worn before, but it was quite suitable for traveling and just a touch stylish. She would appear proper and well-kept but not so posh as to attract unwanted attention. It seemed the infallible Miss Quinton, or Mrs. Black as it were, had quite the natural flair for espionage.

"How long will Samuel be staying with Great Aunt Lydia? I did not get the chance to truly meet the lad, and I would very much like to do so," Sarah said as she met Nora's eyes in the mirror and watched the other's woman's face melt into a smile.

"I daresay we could send for him once we make port in Liverpool. York isn't much farther north. You and Nathan can go fetch him before returning to London if you wish, or perhaps Lydia feels like a visit to town," Jane said.

Sarah made a face, and she watched Nora's barely controlled laugh in the reflection of the mirror.

"I do hope for everyone's sake, Great Aunt Lydia does not feel like a visit to town. We will surely all be in for it then."

"With all of this unsavory talk on the subject of Great

Aunt Lydia, I worry about what my son may be like when next I see him," Nora said.

Jane waved this concern away with the flick of her wrist. "Nonsense, my dear. Nathan and Alec practically grew up at Lydia's and look how they turned out."

"I think that's Nora's concern exactly, Jane," Sarah said just as Nora placed the last pin into her hair.

Nora stepped back and surveyed the work as Sarah continued to watch her in the mirror. There was something not quite right about Nora this morning. The housekeeper was just the slightest touch not herself. It was not as if Sarah could say what it was. It was more just a feeling she had. Sarah obligingly turned her head this way and that to survey the up do herself.

"If you are ever thinking of entering a different profession, Mrs. Black, I could always use a fine lady's maid."

Nora smiled. "A different profession? The last I checked I quit my employ rather abruptly a short time ago. Perhaps you could offer me a profession in the first place."

Sarah shook her head.

"Certainly not, Nora. I am speaking of your career as a spy. You're quite good at it."

Now Nora blushed, and Sarah smiled at the woman's reaction. It wasn't long ago that Nora would not have given a reaction at all, stoic to the last with her housekeeper's training ever in place. But now Nora smiled and blushed and even laughed. Sarah was so happy Nathan had found her. Or perhaps it was the other way around.

And looking back in the mirror at herself, Sarah could say she was glad she had found Alec and that he had found her. For too long, misunderstood words had kept them separated, but now, she knew it would be different. Now she knew, Alec would never be far from her again. With or without words.

And with even greater certainty, she knew he would never leave her.

"What time does the ship leave port?" Sarah asked as she stood, shaking out the skirts of her day gown.

It felt good to be clean and in whole clothes again with petticoats and shifts and tapes and buttons and slippers. She felt complete and normal again and relished the feeling of hair pins against her scalp. Now a hat and reticule would complete the ensemble just nicely, and she could return to being the Countess of Stryden. Only this time, she swore to truly make it her own, and when people said my lady, she would turn her head with the greatest degree of arrogance she could fathom.

"This afternoon, I believe," Jane said, also standing. "But I'm almost certain Richard will want to get there early."

It sounded as though Jane had meant to say more, but her words ended abruptly. Sarah looked up at the older woman only to find her staring at a spot over her shoulder. Sarah turned to where Nora stood a little ways from them in the room.

Nora stood perfectly still, one thin hand pressed to her stomach, her face completely white. And before Sarah could ask if everything were all right, Nora was already headed to the chamberpot and had commenced being sick into it. Sarah and Jane moved together, one grabbing the chamberpot for Nora while the other held the thin woman's shaking shoulders. It was Jane, ever the mother, who spoke first.

"There you go, dear, have it all up. It will do no good to keep it in your stomach."

When it appeared that she had finished, Sarah set down the chamberpot and scurried out of the room in search of something for the poor woman to drink to rid her mouth of the acrid taste of her own stomach contents. She flew into the main room of the suite, completely stalling the conversation that had been occurring at the breakfast table at the far end of the room. The men began to stand at her entrance, but she shooed them back in their seats even as she snatched the tea pot and a cup from the table.

"No, no, nothing amiss here," she said although no one had asked her a single question.

She moved as quickly as the tea pot would allow her, returning to her room and snapping the door closed on the men gathered outside. She poured Nora a cup of tea and brought it to where Jane had made her recline on the settee.

"How long have you felt ill?" Jane asked, and Nora shook her head.

"Oh, it's nothing really. I am sure my stomach is just upset with all the travel. I will be fine as soon as we return to Liverpool."

The statement seemed out of place coming from the stalwart housekeeper, and Sarah poked her. "That's not true, is it? You're carrying a child."

Sarah didn't know where the thought had come from but suddenly it was there, fully formed in her head, and there was nothing she could do for it except to say it out loud.

Jane gasped at the pronouncement, but Nora merely smiled.

"I haven't told Nathan yet. I was only truly sure of it this morning when I woke up feeling this way. It's been like this for the past few days, and I just wanted to be sure before I said something to him."

Sarah's face hurt with the smile that had found its way to her lips. "Oh, Nora, how exciting! Perhaps I could knit little booties for the tyke."

Where on Earth that statement had come from, Sarah had no clue, but Jane looked at her oddly.

"You do not know how to knit and since when are you concerned about little booties?"

Sarah's hand went instinctually to her stomach. Jane did not miss the motion.

"Oh, that is how it is then, I see." Jane stood, heading toward the door. "Both of my sons have finally decided to give me grandbabies, and they decide to try for it at the same time. I am going to be covered in nappies before long."

And with this statement, Jane left the room.

"Are you hoping for a girl, then?" Sarah asked as soon as the door shut.

Nora smiled, and Sarah went on. "You could name her Jane or Lydia. Either would be a most daring choice."

But Nora only smiled more and said, "I was thinking about Sarah for a name."

* * *

ALEC STOOD on the steps of The Owl and Fork Inn with his wife by his side as the Duke of Lofton's carriage approached. The driver would take them to the docks and then depart for London with the duke's carriage while the traveling party proceeded to Liverpool and hopefully, lose any contingent that was still attempting to find them.

He watched the sea breeze play with the tendrils of his wife's hair that hung below her hat and marveled at the normalcy of it. He was just a man standing on the steps of an inn with his wife awaiting a carriage. It was something any gentleman would have taken for granted, but for Alec, it was something he was sure to cherish forever.

Sarah had been quiet since he had left her that morning with Nora. He had told her of what he had learned after speaking with his father, but she had not much to comment on it. She had smiled, of course, and exclaimed her surprise and astonishment at what his mother had done for him. But it was as if she had known his mother would have done such a thing.

So he poked her then, and she turned to him, a smile already on her face when before she surely would have hit him.

"What is it that has your thoughts?" he asked.

Her smile faltered slightly, and he felt a pang of dread at what she might say next.

"It's nothing really," she said, "It's only that there is so much to think about."

Alec watched her face, not really certain what she meant.

"So much to think about?"

The light of the late spring day glanced off of her milky white skin underneath her hat, and Alec wanted to reach up, take her hat and let the sun hit her full in the face just so he could see the way it made her eyes light up. But instead he stood there, holding her arm politely in his as they waited for the carriage to be brought round.

"Yes, there is quite a lot to think on that I had not considered previously, and now it's as though I need to catch up."

Alec raised an eyebrow. "Such as?"

"Children," she said flatly, turning to him, and Alec took an involuntary step away from her, which just brought her with him as he held onto her arm.

"Children?" he said, not enjoying how his voice fluctuated.

"Yes, children." And then her voice grew soft and sad. "Do you not want children, Alec?"

"Oh, it's not that. Of course, I want children. It's just that they're so dirty," he finally decided on saying when in fact he was feeling every kind of repulsion known to him. "Have you ever seen a dirty nappie?"

Sarah laughed, a sparkling sound amongst the cacophony of the daily business of the port town.

"Have you?" she countered, and now Alec, too, had to laugh.

"I can only imagine the horror," he said, which had his wife laughing with greater force.

"But I've never thought of children. What if we've created one? Have you thought of that?"

He raised an eyebrow. "I find that highly unlikely," he said, even though the same thought had come to his mind in a moment of panic on the ship.

Sarah poked him as he had done to her just moments before.

"That's what everyone thinks until all of a sudden you're with child."

Alec turned to look at her fully.

"What has brought on this sudden talk of children?" he said, and he caught the way her eyes moved to the left just as he asked the question.

"Nothing," she said, innocently enough, but he knew something brewed beneath her statement.

He decided to leave it at that and let his wife have her thoughts to occupy her. They had a private suite on board the vessel that would take them to Liverpool, and he planned to use it to the greatest extent that he could. They may have been married for over four years, but this would be the wedding trip they had never had. And he would make the most of it.

"Emily. If we have a girl, I would like to name her Emily," he heard himself say and felt Sarah's eyes upon him.

"I think Emily would be a fine name," she said, and then they both stood on the steps in silence.

The carriage came round with Nathan at the box, but this time, Nora was suspiciously absent.

"She's gone on ahead with Father and Jane to secure the quarters on the ship," Nathan said as he jumped down. "I'm to escort you to the docks, my lord and lady," he said with a flourishing bow.

"Well, see to it that the way is not bumpy, lowly servant, or I shall have your head," Alec said in as gruff a manner as he could manage, but Nathan only laughed at him, pulling open the door to the carriage.

Alec reached for Sarah's hand to help her step up to the carriage, but his wife was oddly missing when he turned around. Panic seized him instantly, and all thought fled his mind even as the breath stopped in his lungs. But then he saw her, just a few steps from him at the edge of the steps of The Owl and Fork Inn, leaning ever so slightly to the side as if to see around something.

"Sarah?" he called, but she did not respond.

He looked at Nathan, who only raised his eyebrows and shook his head.

Alec moved in the direction of his wife, carefully touching her elbow when he reached her to gain her attention. She jumped as if he had startled her, a hand flying to her throat.

"Oh, sorry," she said, and he saw the confusion in her eyes even as she shook her head to clear it, "I thought I saw someone."

Alec looked beyond her but all he saw was an old, crippled dark-skinned man carrying a sack over one shoulder, shuffling off into the distance. He looked back at Sarah.

"Are you all right?" he asked.

And Sarah nodded. "Quite fine."

He took her arm as they went back to the waiting carriage.

"Are you ready for this journey, my wife?" he asked her, and she looked up at him and smiled.

"Always," she said as she took his hand.

CHAPTER 14

*L*ondon, England
June 1815

SHE WATCHED THE CARRIAGES MOVING, counted the beats as the wheels passed in front of her. She heard the switch of the reins and the staccato of the horses' hooves as her own breath mixed with the sound of it all, her heart thumping in time. She was ready to make another try at it when the hand descended on her shoulder, snatching her back.

"You'll get yourself killed if you do it that way," said a voice far above her head, a voice that sounded oddly like that of a refined lady.

Ginny looked up, shielding her eyes with a grimy hand as the sunlight blinded her. But as her eyes adjusted, she saw it was not only a lady that had grabbed her, but a lady with a right fine gentleman hanging onto her arm. Ginny backed up, shaking her shoulder from the woman's grasp.

"And what do ye know of it?" she said, turning to move away, but the woman grabbed her again.

Ginny shook hard to break the woman's grasp, but the woman was stronger than any lady Ginny had ever met.

"I know a thing or two more than you do, and if you'd like to not end up dead, you'll listen to what I have to say."

Ginny stopped moving, feeling an odd sense of respect for this lady growing inside of her.

"A lady like you don't know nothing on it," Ginny said, but her fight was quickly replaced with suspicion.

She didn't know who this lady or her gentleman friend was, but there was something about her that Ginny thought was familiar like. So she stopped trying to break loose and listened to the woman.

The lady carried a parasol made of finer silk than Ginny had ever snitched. Ginny wondered where she'd gotten it and if she perhaps would be able to steal some for herself one day. That would make her a pretty farthing or two even. She could eat like a queen for a whole day. The thought had her salivating. But the lady handed the parasol to the gentleman and, grabbing handfuls of her fine skirt, squatted to the same level as Ginny.

Ginny took a step back, having never had a lady, genteel or otherwise, squat down to her level. The girl looked at the lady, at the woman's clean, golden hair all done up with pretty ribbons and a little square hat that sat in the middle of her head like some kind of crown. At least, that's how Ginny saw it. When Ginny tried to see the color of the woman's eyes, it was then that she noticed the lady was not looking at her. Ginny turned in the direction of the lady's gaze to find she was looking at the traffic just as Ginny had been doing.

"Hackneys are the key to this, you know," the lady said, and Ginny swung around to look at her, mesmerized by the little brackets that formed around her mouth when she spoke.

"Hackneys?" Ginny heard herself say, not really believing that she was speaking with a real lady or that the lady was talking about dodging hackneys with her. This was a lady that Ginny would have cut the purse from as soon as looked at her. And here she was speaking to her. Helping her really.

Ginny looked back at the stream of traffic.

"Hackneys are not as well sprung as the carriages of finer households. You know how to tell the difference, right? In the colors they bear?"

Ginny nodded quickly. "I learned that a while back, but 'ow's it you know that?" Ginny asked, but she didn't take her eyes off of the traffic, so engrossed was she with the lady's words.

"Oh, there was a time when it was necessary," the lady said, her words drifting as she studied the movement before her. "There!" she said, and Ginny jumped with the force of it. But even as she jumped she saw what the lady meant.

It was a hackney, bouncing along with the traffic, but as it moved, she saw the space. There was at least a two beat space between it and the other carriages as it tried to keep up on shoddy springs.

"There's a space," Ginny whispered, and the lady stood up.

"There is, indeed," the lady said.

Ginny watched the hack roll by and saw the distinct clearing left by its wobbling progression. She would be sure to escape unhindered through a hole that size if the need ever arose to quickly lose the authorities that always seemed to plague her.

"Well, what kind of luck do ye need to find one of them to cut through in this 'ere traffic?" Ginny said, pointing to the traffic as the lady stood.

"I wouldn't count on luck, my friend," the lady said, as she retrieved her parasol from the handsome gentleman, "Luck is nothing by which to judge a man or a lady. Intelligence is much more the thing."

And with that, the woman strolled away on the arm of the gentleman, and Ginny was sure she would never again meet such a remarkable lady.

ABOUT THE AUTHOR

Jessie decided to be a writer because the job of Indiana Jones was already filled.

Taking her history degree dangerously, Jessie tells the stories of courageous heroines, the men who dared to love them, and the world that tried to defeat them.

Jessie makes her home in the great state of New Hampshire where she lives with her husband and two very opinionated Basset hounds. For more, visit her website at jessieclever.com.